FIT THE CRIME
The Impostor Lie

CORINNE ARROWOOD

Fit the Crime: The Impostor Lie.
Copyright © 2024 Corinne Arrowood All rights reserved.

Text: Copyright © 2024 by Corinne Arrowood, All rights reserved.

No part of this publication may be reproduced, stored or transmitted in any form or by any means, electronic, mechanical, photocopying, recording, scanning, or otherwise without written permission from the publisher. It is illegal to copy this book, post it to a website, or distribute it by any other means without permission.

This is a work of fiction. Names, characters, places, and incidents, either are the product of the author's imagination or are used fictitiously. Any resemblance to actual persons, living or dead, events, or locales, is entirely coincidental.

Published by Corinne Arrowood
United States of America
www.corinnearrowood.com

ISBN: 978-1-962837-06-4 (eBook)
ISBN: 978-1-962837-07-1 (Trade Paperback)
ISBN: 978-1-962837-08-8 (Hardcover)

Cover and Interior Design by Cyrusfiction Productions.

TABLE OF CONTENTS

Days to Months	1
Less Than You	15
One to Another	29
This for That	43
Wake From Slumber	63
Back To Business	73
Wrong Place, Wrong Time	85
Big Plans	99
Bleak Soul	115
Nothing But the Truth	129
Chestnut Bound	139
Heads or Tails	153
Home at Last	167
Many Thanks	181
Other Books by the Author	185
About The Author	186

A Special Note

The statistics of PTSD are staggering. Many of our Marines and soldiers come home entrenched in the horrors they experienced and the nightmares they cannot escape. If you know one of our heroes that might be suffering from PTSD, contact Wounded Warrior Project, National Center for PTSD, VA Caregiver Support Line at 888-823-7458.

The Impostor Lie

DAYS TO MONTHS

*O*ut of nowhere, a thrash of blonde hair whipped around, and massive hands with purple enameled fingernails clawed into her arm; the woman was all over her. "You fuckin' bitch," the woman screamed at her as she picked her up and flung her into the wall, then shook her like a ragdoll, her head pounding against the tile. There was no time to be afraid; the lights went out. Voices echoed in the distance from all directions. "Hold on, Missy," an EMT coached. Babe's voice overpowered all of them, "Trinity, fight. I got you." She remembered commands to drive faster and the piercing sound of sirens. "She's crashing." Then darkness enveloped her like a shroud. It was as though she were living in someone else's nightmare. Strange sounds and hollowed-out voices merged into a reverberation of nonsensical utterances, like being on a carousel and hearing every tenth word someone said within the frolicking melody of an organ. Then, a peaceful embrace lifted her as though she were floating. It was serene, a heavenly dream; Babe's voice fractured the tranquility, "Stay with me," he commanded. Nightmares came and went, and there was no today or any particular moment in time; it was just a figment of somebody else.

Trinity's eyes twitched back and forth in an unconscious state of agitation, and the monitors started beeping at an alarming rate, sending signals that something was desperately wrong. Antoinette slid the door with force, screaming amidst tears. "Help my baby somebody. Oh God, no, no, no." The staff burst into the room, pushing Antoinette and Antoine aside. They brought the cart in to shock her heart back into rhythm. A nurse turned to them and instructed them to leave the room. She heard more than once the team was losing her. Her parents stood outside the sliding glass door for what seemed eons yet didn't tell Babe; they knew how despondent he was. The frenzy calmed, and a rhythmic beat settled in the air. Antoinette, being let back in, kissed Trinity on the forehead. "Sleep my baby."

They came from the ICU; Antoine had his arm around her mom's shoulder. Antoinette's eyes streaked with tears, but she had regained composure. Whatever the crisis, it was over. He didn't know how much more his heart could take. It seemed there was something cataclysmic every day, and no matter what, they excluded him from the involvement as though he didn't exist. It was the nurses that kept him informed. Over and over, he thought, *Where are your miracles, God?*

Months rolled around in the blink of an eye, but to Babe, each day was painstaking drudgery and heartbreak. Little by little, Trinity's physical condition improved, according to the doctors. Babe's role was still in a murky void. Each day was different; she mostly remained unconscious, maintaining vitals within normal limits. However, now and then, she'd mutter something indistinguishable, occasionally opening her glassed-over eyes and staring at nothing.

Babe waited patiently, and his heart ached every time he saw her. On the rare occurrence when her eyes were open, she looked with emptiness. How could she not remember all their great times, how he'd been her hero, how they'd laughed like school kids and the passionate times as lovers? He could recall all their interludes. He prayed to her God, and while some of the prayers came true, why wouldn't this supposedly loving God open her mind to the happiness they had shared? The demons tore at him, shredding his heart, reminding him she didn't remember because he didn't deserve her love. How much more could he bear?

He couldn't carry on feeling useless; it wasn't part of his DNA. It was time to make some decisions. He found he'd spent more and more time at home with the boys and away from the hospital. He was nothing more than a giant anchor weighing the situation. The boys had difficulty understanding how Trinity couldn't remember Babe. People who only met him once remembered him; he was memorable at six foot five, with a wall of rippled muscle and intensity from his eyes, similar to Superman with his x-ray vision. Marines stationed with him remembered him even if they hadn't been part of his unit. He was a testament to the Marines' finest and most courageous. He was a legend, a figure many stood in awe of, yet his wife had no memory of their relationship. God was cruel.

Babe called a meeting with Antoine, her father.

The big man hadn't planned what he would say to Antoine; maybe he was looking for guidance. He entered Hotel Noelle and took the elevator to the office. Rose Marie, with her bright pink lips and sparkling teeth, looked at him with pity when he entered. Her usual beaming smile had all but disappeared. "He's waiting for you, darlin'. That baby of yours is precious. They showed me pictures. Eight pounds eleven ounces is a big baby for tiny Trinity. She's beautiful. So heartfelt to name her after Chance; Miss Chancée has your beautiful blue eyes and long black lashes."

"Yes, ma'am." His smile was empty, and anyone could see it. The big man was hurting and totally at a loss. It felt like someone had tightened a vice around his heart; the pain was past the point of bearing.

Antoine stepped out, "Come in, Babe, please." The mood was somber.

Babe entered and stood in front of the chair until Antoine sat and invited him to sit. "Sir, I am perplexed, to be candid. My brother tells me to hang in, but maybe this is the best way Trinity sees to get out of our marriage. I don't want to hold her to something she doesn't want. I haven't been hanging around the hospital because I feel useless, and the boys need me. I go to the nursery to see the baby; Chancée relaxes in my arms as I rock her."

Babe sat with his feet flat on the floor, hands on his thighs, the same position he had sat in for weeks on end in the hospital waiting room. When he accepted he couldn't help, he knew three kids at home who needed him desperately. Since the "Who are you?" Trinity hadn't communicated with Babe. Those were her last words before edging closer to death. He saw her eyes roll back like her spirit gave way to the angels. Of all the things to say and the last words he might ever hear from her. She had ripped his heart out and trampled all over it. *Who am I? I'm the man who will love you to the end of time; I'll lay down my life for you. I'm your husband and the one you called your superhero. Isn't there some memory left of us?* He couldn't be angry at her for not remembering.

Antoine tapped his thumb on his desk as though trying to come up with the appropriate words. "Marine, I believe it will all come back one day, but I know you must get on with your life. We're praying, and I suggest you keep praying. In the meantime, you have to fill your life with purpose." He steepled his hands, eyes locking on Babe's soul. "You have to move on, son. The doctors say she could be a ticking time bomb. If something happens with recovery, she could develop a bleed and be gone from us, just like that." He snapped his fingers. "You, Marine, need a life." Babe lowered his head, trying to breathe. "I have a colleague who owns a private military company. They handle big contract clients of national and international importance. I told him about you, and he is interested in meeting with you. The contracts are not lengthy. We will apprise you of any changes, but you should move on. Any progress, I will make it easy to get you home," he said. "It's legit."

Babe's mind returned to other operations and remembered thinking *if they say something is legit, know it probably isn't. If something's legit, one doesn't have to qualify; it just is. Legit is the norm. It's a bit like bragging about never having been to prison. Stupid fucker, you're not supposed to be incarcerated.* Their conversation ended with Babe saying he'd think about it. He weighed the option of contacting Jarvis and helping their cause. It was making a change and a worthy one. Babe left Hotel Noelle, none the wiser. *What a waste of time.*

Working at the job site had become ancient history, yet he wondered how progress was coming. Perhaps he'd pass by for a quick minute. His mind was a whirlwind of what-ifs. *C'mon God, give me a sign.*

The trill of his phone snapped him to the present, and, while suckworthy, it was his reality.

"Vicarelli," he answered, taking long strides toward his truck.

"Hello, sweetheart. Antoine told me you just left his office. Can you come to the house? It's important." Trinity's mom's voice didn't indicate trembles of worry or hitches of tears, but he detected a level of significance.

Babe picked up his pace. "Yes, ma'am. I'm on my way."

"Darlin', no need to speed." Antoinette always played the role of a mother. How nice it would have been to have a strong mother and not one that had been beaten so far into submission that she was a mere facsimile of herself. Nonetheless, he loved his mother and wished he'd known her better. Still, in all, Antoinette and Antoine attempted to fill a void despite going through their Hell. Trinity was their baby, and after losing Chance, it was a miracle they could handle the situation so well, still willing to extend warmth to him. It was kind of them.

Was his absence at the hospital his way of moving on? He'd go every few days, checking on her, but mostly to spend time with Chancée. His visits were gradually getting more infrequent. He no longer sat hour upon hour in the waiting room. He'd pop his head in, kiss her hand or forehead, stop by the nursery to see his baby, and head back home. The heavy-weight bag had noticeable signs of wear and tear. His weightlifting had gotten extreme, and his morning or evening runs had increased to ten or fifteen miles. He drowned himself in physical fitness activities and played hoops with the boys. The four men of the house, as he referred to them, had become an identifiable family. He was a dad with three sons. Babe was tired of being in the dark, so he figured he'd mind the homefront and stay away from the hospital for a few days until he decided to talk with Antoine. The day had come, a meeting planned, and he was still in the dark after it. Was there something no one told him? Antoine should have had the answers, man to man. His mind drifted, dragging his emotions with each memory, making the drive to her parents almost torturous. What did Antoinette want? Was she going to tell Babe to move on? Did someone have a plan for Trinity that he was unaware of? He pulled up to the house and drew a deep breath; the urge to vomit was almost non-negotiable. He didn't want to move on; he wanted her back again.

Walking into the Noelle house was like entering a florist shop. Flowers of condolences for Chance's death and Trinity's attack continued to flood in. Once a week, or more often if required, Mama Noelle would have her house help drive the arrangements to nursing homes, hospitals, and rehabilitation centers. Nonetheless, the pungent aroma of flowers had permeated their home.

As he approached the door, Antoinette welcomed him in. She led him to the den. He couldn't believe his eyes; Trinity sat in a ball under blankets on the sofa, surrounded by baby paraphernalia. She was awake; why hadn't anyone called him? Why hadn't Antoine divulged that important fact, maybe trying to get him out of the picture? It had been less than half an hour since he had sat in front of Antoine's desk hearing about possible contract work, yet the man had said nothing about Trinity being at his house. It had only been a few days since Babe had seen her at the hospital. Last he saw, she was still like Sleeping Beauty. Here, she was awake and smiling, even though slightly hollow. What happened to the transparency and 'we'll let you know of any changes immediately?' He puzzled again. *Strange. Why hadn't they told me they moved her to their house? Fucking people.*

"Hey, Vic," she crooned, "Come sit next to me." Babe could hardly believe his ears. It was the first time she acknowledged him by name since the tragedy. Now, she knew who he was. He sat. His body was stiff like a toy soldier waiting for the other shoe to drop. "I wanted to talk with you. We'll have to start from the beginning; maybe that'll stir my memories. Could you tell me about our first conversation, like at the bar? I understand I'm a bartender at Louie's Tap." She turned both her palms up, looking for confirmation.

Babe inhaled deeply, his heart swelling with hope. He turned to face her, looking into her eyes. Something was off with her eyes; perhaps it was the loss of sparkle. "I've never been a big talker, and while you are always up for conversation—"

She interrupted, "Were." *What the fuck is going on? Point taken, yes were.*

After months of silence, still on death's doorstep only a few days previously now, she'd left the hospital and was talking a mile a minute. Something was not right; it didn't add up. He nodded, taking in another deep breath. *Don't fuck this up, Vicarelli,* he reinforced his will. He cleared his throat, "I gave you my order, a two-finger pour—"

"Of Glenlivet, right?" She moved closer to him, staring face to face. He studied her every move and facial expression; he didn't remember light freckles across her nose. They were barely noticeable, maybe always covered with makeup, but he didn't remember her freckled, even in their many interludes in the shower.

A slight sparkle returned to his eyes, "Yes, ma'am. You asked me, 'your two fingers or mine?'"

She laughed and asked, "Really?" He nodded. "Keep going, Vic." What was it with her voice? Had it always sounded so nasally? Maybe it was from swelling. He was looking at her, but she wasn't there.

For the next half hour, he told the story. Trinity laughed a few times. "So, I came onto you like gangbusters, you say. You probably thought I was some easy—"

It was his turn to interrupt, "No, ma'am. Never. Trinity, you were and are the most beautiful and precious person to me." He leaned into the conversation, reading her every expression and nuance. She was trying; she wanted to make it happen and revive their relationship. *Maybe we have hope.*

She tucked her legs under her, giving her a few more inches of height on the couch, still looking up in his direction. "I get clips like reels on Facebook. Most of them have us," she looked down and whispered, "naked." Babe nodded. "I mean, did we screw all the time?" She tipped her head to the side in curiosity.

His heart burst as his face blushed with a look like the cat-that-ate-the-canary. "We made love. You are my first girlfriend." She slapped his arm, saying no way. He smiled and nodded, acknowledging that other physical interactions had satisfied an urge but no girlfriends.

"So, like, prostitutes?" He shrugged a shoulder while tipping his head slightly, confirming the answer. She scratched her head; her mind drifted somewhere. " Did I—" she looked in the direction of the kitchen.

"You cut my hair, and we had an adventure of sorts in your parents' half bath." He pointed in the direction of the kitchen, but was that what she was referring to? *Maybe, maybe not. Odd memory if it was.*

She apologized for not recognizing him initially and saying who are you; obviously, he was a big part of her life. Bethany, her older sister, had suggested starting with him in familiar territory. She took his hand and led him in the direction of her bedroom. It was a most uncomfortable position she'd put him in. It wasn't that he didn't desire her, but it smacked of rape since she wasn't in her right mind. He pulled back. "Please," she asked. Did she want to quench a need, or was she genuinely hoping it would reconnect them? "Look, Vic, this isn't just a booty call if that's what you're thinking. Bethany said maybe if we connected in well-practiced territory, I might start remembering more. The quick blips I have seem to follow her idea, but every now and then, I see—" she looked away. "Some sort of violence, but not toward me. Have you protected me a lot?" She held his hands, walking backward toward her room, pulling him along. Her progress was unbelievable, having been noncommunicative three days prior. *Miracles, God?*

By this time, they'd reached her bedroom door. She led Babe inside. He leaned down and whispered, "May I kiss you?" She lunged forward and kissed him, turning the sweet kiss into one of passion. "Wait. You are not well enough to play in the sheets. You just woke up from death's doorstep, and I sure as shit don't want to put you at risk." She let her clothes fall to the floor as she undid his belt and pulled at his jeans. Babe was scared to hurt her. He sat on her bed, naked and most uncomfortable. It all felt strange to him. She climbed into his lap. His eyes closed, "Oh, girl," he exhaled as she rubbed her body next to his. "I've missed you, but—" she put a finger over his lips. Being with him in this manner resonated with her, as well. She tilted her head; he thought he saw the sparkles of memory burst in her eyes, or was it something he wanted to see?

It looked as if Trinity remembered being in his arms, her body moving with his like she had loved the man intensely, but the once firey feeling was only a quick flame, like striking a match. The tinder to alight and stoke the blaze was missing. Then, with the finale, she dismissed him like their passion was over but curiously asked, "Can you come back tomorrow? Being with you was great, and the memories are beginning to click." *Warning, red flags.* She was different, no doubt, and he was confused.

Still bewildered by the totality of the situation, he answered, "I'll be here. What time?" He pondered a thought and went for it, tiptoeing on the ledge, exposing his heart. "Do you want to see the boys this weekend? Maybe come home for a bit?"

Trinity sat upright, looking at his face, trying to get a read. She seemed perplexed. "I am home." Period, no discussion. "Vic, are you saying we have other children, and I live somewhere else?"

Then the next thought hit him like a sledgehammer; she parroted rehearsed lines from Bethany. Still naked in bed with her, while it was pleasing, the idea crushed his soul. Their interaction hadn't been authentic, more like a theatrical performance. It was as natural as it got on his part but not hers. "Trinity, why do you call me Vic?"

She pulled on a lock of hair like a child caught in a lie. "Because that's your name." It came out more like a question.

He turned on his side, petting her arm. He used the most gentle voice he could find. "Is that what Bethany told you to call me?" Trapped in the headlights with exaggerated blinks, would she reveal her old nature or come out with something even more bizarre? Trinity had always been honest, brutally so. Had that changed?

She bent her head into her chest. "Y-yes. Is that not your name?" The tears began to fall.

"Oh, ma girl, no need to cry." He wiped a tear from her cheek and held her close. "My name is Babe, and you sometimes called me Vic, but mostly Babe, Vicarelli, or Big Man." He began his life story, not missing a step. If she wanted to rekindle the magic of them, it had to be from the beginning. If the love sparked to life, it was real; if not, come what may. He sat up against the headboard; she rested alongside him, entranced in every word. Her brow crinkled, and eyes became glossy while he talked about the abuse as a boy, but then she opened them wide when Babe admitted to shattering his father's shoulder. "We need to get dressed; this is a long ass story, and I'm sure your mother will start wondering what's going on in here. I'm sure she has a clue, but with potential brain bleeds, I don't want her to think we are overdoing things; besides, you seemed to dismiss me after the big hurrah, anyway, like I was a one-and-done. Even the working girls talked more."

They returned to the den after getting dressed. He talked about school, wrestling, college, and the Marines. "So, you're some badass Marine man?"

He grinned, "I don't know about the badass, but I'm pretty good in a scuffle." Storytime was the perfect opportunity to eliminate the lives he'd taken and told her about previously, but what about honesty? The more gruesome stories would hold for another time as a means of self-preservation. Would she have the social barometer to keep such things confidential? So far, he felt like a means to an end, not that he didn't relish being in her arms, but the encounter was purely physical on her part. Did it genuinely seem like a plan to ignite her memory? *Maybe, but something is amiss. It's nothing new that she likes to play in bed,* he reminisced.

Babe brought her up to speed with the adoption of Gunner. "Where is he? So, you broke the guy's arm because he was mean to his dog?" He nodded, desperately wanting to say at least he hadn't killed the motherfucker. Given the chance again, he might eliminate the threat, not merely neutralize it for a moment. He went into what he felt was his mission in life: fighting for those who were too weak to fight, and left it there.

She rested against the arm of the couch, putting her feet in his lap. Instinctively, he began kneading her feet. "I do remember this," she smiled. He watched as memories seemed to pop into her head, overflowing like popcorn at the movies; they kept pouring out. "I have a place attached to my family's hotel and a house in Lakeview—" as though plucking pictures from her subconscious, then stood on the couch with fistsful of hair, expounding as though a discovery. The light had switched on to a particular memory. She pointed at him, "You saved me from my ex-brother-in-law, oh my God. He raped me, didn't he, and beat me up," the tears started flowing into sobs, "Jesus, he's a sicko, but you found me and saved me." Her eyes became round as in a sketch done by a caricaturist; she dropped to a crouch on the sofa and whispered, "You killed him, didn't you, to save me?"

Babe's face sombered. He said he was sorry she remembered that, but she reiterated it was to save her and how much he must love her to risk the danger and prison. She asked if her dad knew, then said of course he knew, and it was no wonder her parents loved him so much.

Mama Noelle entered the den with a bowl of grapes. Trinity started talking; Babe took her hand and squeezed it lightly. She cocked her head with an expression that said, give me some credit. "Mama, I am remembering a bunch, and what I don't, Vic is filling in the gaps. We've only gotten a little way, but it's a start." The mother-daughter combo chatted for a while, although he felt more like being in a theatre. Running through his mind was where their relationship would go from there. Did she want friends with benefits? He didn't think he could do that. She held the key to his heart, and if she didn't want to be his wife or have him involved in Chancée's life, then it wouldn't work. He wasn't anyone's play toy, not even the tiny Miss Trinity.

Odd emotions went through him; it was akin to pissed but not, hurt but not. Watching the animated overacting didn't have the slightest resemblance to the woman he loved. Trinity was authentic; what you saw is what you got, kind of girl. If this were the new version, it'd be better to bow out. Babe didn't blame her for the amnesia or personality change; he merely grieved for the Trinity from before. Part of him wished he could dig up Markey's psycho sister-brother tag team and torture them to death over and over; they stole her from him, and the duo dying once wasn't enough. Inez, Paul and he suspected a few of the farm hands pounded the piss out of them before elimination. Babe felt sure there were two new unmarked graves to add to the many others.

"Well?" she asked. "What do you think?"

"About what?" His thoughts had taken him down a rabbit hole, and he missed some conversation. He hoped it wasn't vital.

Trinity seemed a little irritated. "Will you pick me up tomorrow, and I can see your dog and sons?"

"Of course, but they are ours. I'll be here about noon; we'll pick up lunch, go to the house, and play with Gunner. Ruthie has been itching to hold the baby. Then, the boys should get home from school, but we have to talk. I've explained where Gunner came from, but we haven't touched on the boys. There's a long explanation there. By the way, I have pieces and parts for the nursery, which is off our bedroom, but I haven't put them all together. We'll make it a team effort." She blankly stared at him. *Or maybe we won't. What the fuck is going on?*

"Okay." She finally responded but had little to no expression in her voice. The baby's room didn't seem to interest her. *Strange.*

Mama Noelle returned to the den with Chancée. Babe stood and held out his arms before she sat. Trinity's mother beamed and put the baby in his arms. He sat, one leg crooked on the other, providing a natural cradle for the baby. He whispered to her, touching her silken skin along her face. He was at ease with her. Comfortable was an insufficient description. The interaction was far more than that; it was a spiritual connection between him and his baby girl. The baby looked at his face, zeroing in on his eyes. There was the look of awe and wonder. He hummed a sweet lullaby to her.

Trinity interrupted, "You sing? Do you dance? W-wait, you sang to me, remember?"

"He only slow dances, Trinity. Don't you remember telling me that at the wedding?" Her mother interjected; she replied she remembered. The thought glanced through his mind, or *does she?*

He smiled and nodded. He remembered how shocked she was when he sang to her. There was nothing wrong with his memory; it was memory-worthy. Trinity appeared shocked. He held the baby, stroking her tiny fingers for half an hour. The baby made sounds a few times but didn't cry; she was perfectly content in her father's arms. "It must be close to feeding time," he commented. Trinity said he could feed her. Rather than ask about breastfeeding, he didn't want to pick a wound.

"I'll go get a bottle. I imagine they are in the kitchen." She told him to sit and that she would find one. *Find one?*

Things were most unnatural between Trinity and the baby. She asked if she breastfed the boys. He answered no, and it was a long story. She began with a barrage of questions: Were they from a previous marriage? What happened to their mother? Why was he taking care of them; was she unfit? "Trinity, it's a long explanation, but basically, I rescued them from being trafficked; I was late on Jacob, but he's with us now." Her mouth was tightly closed. If he had to describe her facial expression, it would range between embarrassed and ashamed. "It's okay, you didn't remember."

She gently felt the shaved area of her hair in the back from where they had surgically put her back together. Fortunately, she had enough hair for two or three people and could cover the healing scar. Trinity patted her hair with her fingers and braided it down one side. "How's this look?" She turned her head so he could look from all angles. "Shit, you rescued those boys. You are an amazing man." He responded that he loved her hair; it was always a favorite way she wore it. She looked surprised. *It's brain trauma; I've seen it before.* The thought brought Kevin Kelly to mind. *He was perhaps the most foul-mouthed, rough person he'd been around, and that was saying something with his unit. A grenade went off and sent him flying. His head took the brunt of his landing. When he awoke after being comatose for weeks, he was soft-spoken and timid. The absence of foul words was shocking. The change was permanent; the Corps gave him a medical discharge.* Trinity's peculiar behavior wasn't quite as drastic but still off-target. Would she be like Kelly, and this was it, or would she return to herself?

Babe couldn't believe his thoughts; he was ready to leave and unsure about this new Trinity. It certainly wasn't the woman he fell in love with. Did he even like her? He fed the baby and, when finished, mentioned he had to go. "Please, no, I've missed you." His mind whirred; *how can you miss someone you don't know? She indicated earlier for me to leave. This is a monumental cluster fuck.*

"You sure about that?" he asked.

She copped an attitude, "Yes, what, you don't believe me? You think I'm lying?" *Definitely not a Trinity answer, she woulda said 'fuck you, Vicarelli!'* The more time he spent with her, the more he didn't like her. *Time to go.*

LESS THAN YOU

The puzzlement and confusion built like stacks of bricks as he drove to Chestnut. Babe had a mound of uncertainty. He loved Trinity with everything he had, at least, the old Trinity. It wasn't her fault what happened to her, and they did vow, for better or worse, in sickness and in health, richer or poorer, until death parted them. If he looked at the whole picture, had he gone straight to Louie's, he might have prevented the beating, but if she had listened to him and stayed home, there would have been no danger. When had she listened to anybody? There was a reason his gut told him to turn around. No, he couldn't and wouldn't bear the guilt of the tragedy. Turning it even further back, had Glenn not hired Markey, there wouldn't even be an enchilada, half or whole.

Ruthie knew the torture he'd gone through with her not remembering him. She'd pat his hand and say give it time, comparing the amnesia to his visions. Everyone who knew him knew it was best not to call it PTSD when, in fact, it was the unspoken truth, and he knew it. The phone buzzed.

"Hey, little brother. How goes it? Her memory coming back yet?" Did he want to go through a lengthy explanation with Mays, his newfound older brother? No. Simple would be better.

"I think she's coming out of the fog, but I'm not sure it's her memories or suggestions from her family. She's not herself yet. Pulling into the house; talk later." Fact: He didn't want to talk, not to anyone. He had had everything: a happy marriage, a fabulous wife, a daughter, and three rambunctious boys. Now, it was as though his life had evaporated. Fact:

Life was one big cluster. He was raging inside, getting ready to burst at the seams.

He pulled into the driveway, got out of the truck, and went to the heavy bag, Fuck the tape, fuck the gloves. He took off his shoes and began to whale. He slugged harder and harder, swept upward, punishing kicks; for sure, whoever the opponent was, he was beating the life out of them. Was he imagining Markey and her family of loonies or God? What did Father O'Shea tell him? God has big shoulders. Just when he started to appreciate the God entity, it got blown to Hell. Why would God do this? If He were the maker of all things and held the reins, He would have seen Trinity as a good Catholic girl. No matter what, she had always given credit to God—not so with Trinity 2.0.

Babe didn't hear Jacob enter the garage. "Jesus, you're bleeding, sir." He stopped momentarily and looked at his raw, swollen, bruised knuckles. Sweat poured off of him in buckets. The soles of his feet were scuffed and red with abrasions. "Are you okay, sir?" The boy looked him over from head to foot. Babe's clothes stuck to his body, which brought on the image of Trinity removing her drenched clothes after work. It was a slick, almost plastic sound or maybe a vacuum-sealed item, requiring force and wit to remove. That's who he wanted most desperately, his wife, the authentic Trinity he'd lusted for night after night in Louie's. She had been the hot minx he'd conjured as he showered. Sometimes he felt like a pubescent lad, finding the pleasure purpose of his pecker. Imagining her in his shower, the two coupled in raw intimacy provided more fulfillment than the talents of a working girl.

Chris barreled into the garage, took one look at the big guy, and expounded, "Fuck me. I never want to get on your wrong side. You look possessed, dude. Reg wasn't far behind; all he could do was stand with his mouth agape at first sight.

"Uh, sir, Ruthie told me to let you know dinner is almost done; she's waiting for the bread to crisp." Reg turned up his hands. "Whatcha want me to tell her? She'll freak if she sees you all bloody." They both stood starkly still, full of observation and question.

Babe relaxed his shoulders and caught his breath. "Boys, y'all go back inside. One of you bring me a big bowl with ice and a dishcloth." He leaned against his grandfather's car and mopped his face with his shirt; he missed the old guy something fierce. He took inventory of the damage he'd done to his body. *Yeah, Ruthie isn't gonna be happy.*

His phone buzzed; it was Antoine, and he'd heard about the day and supposed recognition. "Marine, my girls meant no disrespect. Bethany wants her sister back and life to be normal again, so she fed her information. Who knows if I'll ever have my baby back? This spoiled, entitled person isn't my girl. I understand y'all have plans for tomorrow. I'll talk to you when you pick up Trinity in the morning." The call was to the point, brief, and over. He was getting used to the ways of the Noelles.

Sirens started going off in his head. Antoine wanted him to do something for him. If he set a precedent, then it would be like a life of bondage. After the ice and cleaning up with a dishcloth, Babe was more presentable for dinner. He grabbed a shirt out of the laundry. Ruthie would undoubtedly pitch an almighty fit, and he'd get a scolding. If anything, her doling-out reprimands and the daily routine of the house were the only familiar hooks to hang his hat besides Gunner and the boys. Nothing had changed there.

The aroma of gumbo filled the air, teasing his taste buds. Ruthie called from the kitchen. "I saw your truck; where you go off to?" She ladled the bowls for the boys and snatched the bread out at the perfect time. "You three, come get your dinner. Sir, take a seat, and I'll bring yours in shortly." Like pigs to a trough, the boys hustled in for their bowls, and Ruthie followed close behind. She screeched, "Merciful God, what happened to your hands? Lemme take a look."

Babe explained they were fine; he'd worked out on the heavyweight bag to rid himself of pent-up frustration. The boys were themselves boastful, full of shit, but funny, all with proper manners, a la Ruthie. Babe sat in silence. No sooner had they finished dinner than Ruthie ushered the boys upstairs for showers. She grilled him on Trinity, and he responded with an open heart and truthful thoughts. He played it back and forth between

Trinity's reality versus the past, all the while playing the Devil's Advocate, trying to justify his feelings. He went to the alcohol cabinet, poured a tumbler of Glenlivet, and sat back down, waiting for Ruthie's words of wisdom.

Wait seemed to be the concurrent theme with everyone near and dear. Did Ruthie, his brother, Antoine, and her mom think Trinity would poof snap out of it? He'd rather not be married than live in sheer misery. He'd lived a painful existence as a boy and teen, like the saying, been there, done that, and had the scars to prove it. Babe shared with Ruthie that Trinity was coming to the house the next day. He hoped it might trigger some recollection, but probably not. The big guy would make a point of telling her he'd prefer her not to remember than regurgitate fed information, no matter how good-intentioned. He knew she had to be scared. What if someone stole his memories? Sometimes, he wished specific memories would get erased forever. Coming from the point of fear might be the way to her authenticity. She needed to meet her fears head-on and speak them aloud. That would be plan A, and if it didn't work, then fuck any chances on plans B and C. His best results were always pure reactionary and authentic.

Babe's mind ticked over as he lay in bed, thinking about a possible future. If he did a favor for Antoine, then there would be no indebtedness on his part; it would be the opposite. Maybe having an ace in the hole would be a good thing.

While in his sea of confusion, Trinity called.

"Hi, it's me." Her voice sounded like a frightened child. "I want you to know I desperately want to remember our life together. Mama gave me our wedding album, and we looked happy. I want that back but don't know how to get there. There's been talk about hypnosis. One of Mama's friends said it worked for her son. Somewhere inside of me, I think there are things you've shared with me that you wouldn't want other people to know, maybe soldier things." *Soldier things?*

He interjected, "Marine never soldier. I can take you to the hypnotist if you want. Yes, I have told you things, very private, personal things, but if they slip out while you are under hypnosis, it doesn't matter; we have spousal privilege. Do you remember what that is?" He stopped for a second. His body reacted to some of the things he had shared with her. The film in his mind rolled to the guy in the gas station who smacked his girlfriend around in the car, and he could picture as he followed them and parked next to the POS. *How could making love to Trinity illicit a similar feeling to torquing a neck? They were both powerful primal feelings.* His body responded, and he desperately needed her then."Tell me you love me, Trinity, and want me." His silence was deafening.

Trinity questioned, "Of course, I love you and think I have proven I want you. I want you so much it hurts. To be in your arms is the one thing I can hold onto. What you do to my body sends chills to my core. Do you want me as bad as I want you right now?" Silence, then a moan, "Are you still there? Are you okay?"

He heard himself answer with a sated voice, "Yes, ma'am." He gathered himself and said, "Looking forward to it."

"Me too, Babe Vicarelli." He smiled at her response. She was trying to get back, but there was an underlying current of dishonesty plaguing him.

Having a bit more calm, he assembled the crib and decked it out with linens Ruthie had selected, laundered, and folded. He hung the curtains, which coordinated with everything in the room. Babe hoped Trinity would approve of a Princess theme. The furniture was antique white with painted gold edges and a flicker of gold dust; it looked antique but wasn't. Ruthie had selected everything from furniture to clothes, blankets, and the sundry needed for a baby. She had washed the tiny garments and folded them, ready to put away. He loaded the drawers, attached a mobile to the crib, set the princess lamp on top of the dresser, hung a mirror his grandfather had in the attic, and quickly assembled a changing table. Trinity could put the finishing touches.

After admiring his work, it was shower time. Talking to himself aloud, "I hope I didn't just waste a few grand and set some high hopes." Whether they stayed together or not, he hoped she would visit with the boys and Ruthie with Chancée.

Morning came, and he was back to his exercise routine. Along the way, he passed the kids' friend's house, where the mom, Jane, gave a twinkly smile and fluttery wave. Babe's mind recalled Trinity's response to the neighbor, which made him chuckle. He wanted her back to normal; what they had wasn't perfect, but it was perfect for him. She was hard-headed, sassy, and exuberant with life. She exuded hot, sexy energy. Taming his thoughts, he picked up the pace, thinking of showering, dressing, and driving to speak with Antoine and pick up Trinity. Both interactions were unknown, mysterious, and unnerving. *New feeling*, he acknowledged. He felt jittery, like too much caffeine. *Get the lead out. Marine!*

After a quick shower and drive to Swan Street, he stood at the door with nerves of the unknown. He knocked on the front door. Trinity's voice rang out, "It's open." She was halfway to him when he came inside. She wrapped her arms around his waist and squeezed. She pulled his head toward her. "Hey, give me some sugar," she smiled with a typical, coy, flirty smile. He kissed her with a quick peck. She frowned, "My parents are in the other room; now I want a real kiss." The image zoomed him back to the first time they made love, and the same kind of kiss happened at the crowning moment. *That's so Trinity; maybe I'm wrong.*

Babe grabbed her butt, picked her up. Immediately, she wrapped her legs around him. Things felt great and normal as if nothing had changed. "Intense kiss, lady. I gotta settle down before talking to your dad."

"Better idea," she jumped down, grabbed his hand, led the way to her room, shut and locked the door. "Let me fulfill the fantasy." He started to protest, "My house, my rules!" He laid back on her bed.

"Oh, ma girl, some things just come naturally to you, and this is one."

After she finished, she jumped on top of him. "Babe, it's all coming back, or at least some things. I know you're going out of town for my dad. You and someone else he knows, I heard him on the phone. Your leaving feels all too familiar; I think it happened a lot." She rolled off of him, smoothed her hair, and adjusted her clothes while he took care of other business before seeing her dad. They left the room and walked to the den. She had a pile of baby things to take for the day, one being a car seat for his truck.

Antoine came into the den and asked Babe to follow him.

Babe sat, feet on the floor, hands on his thighs. Her father had a piping hot cup of coffee on his desk. The rising steam was visible from where he sat. Antoine smiled at the big guy and commented that Trinity seemed better after their visit the day prior.

"I don't know what you said to her, but she's not acting demanding and spoiled. My children have had a good life with everything they needed, but they have always worked once they were old enough to drive. Trinity and Chance," he crossed himself, "being the youngest, were not as disciplined as the others, but never have any of our children acted like spoiled brats, and I'm afraid Trinity has shown her ass since starting her recovery. Enough said." He dusted his hands yet came across as cagey. "I have a business associate from the Democratic Republic of the Congo. He is in Mobutu Tenzeki's circle of confidantes. Tenzeki is their President. There has always been a measure of political unrest, but his Prime Minister Zama Sakonde, who has a longer name, but that is the name he goes by, was abducted by one of the Rebel factions. They seem to think he is too progressive and encourages a more Western lifestyle. You must understand that the Congo has many urban areas; however, they vastly differ from ours. In many ways, it is a very backward country and, in some cases, primitive. This is a tremendous problem in the Congo. The President spoke to my friend, who I told you about; he owns a private military contract company. Mobutu contacted William Tazar, owner of Worldwide Security Movement, WSM, who, in turn, contacted me. I have mentioned you a few times in conversation. Bill is a generous person who rewards people who work for him. I cannot lie; this requires nerves of steel and courage, which you have displayed. French is their first language." He looked over the top of his glasses, once again balancing on his nose.

Babe shifted in his chair, "Sir, I am familiar with the Congo, however, I don't speak any of their languages. You must know this assignment will more than likely be a lengthy proposition. Are you prepared for me to be away from your daughter and granddaughter for an extended time? I'm talking, more than likely, weeks, if not months." He looked directly into Antoine's eyes. What he proposed was finding a needle in a haystack. They had nothing to go on, and given the nature of malcontents, the man was probably dead unless they were bargaining for something; he didn't say the words but was thinking them. *Shit, they're more inhumane than some of Javier's compadres; um, second thought, maybe not.*

Squinting his eyes while sipping his boiling coffee, Antoine stared straight at Babe. "My wife makes a strong cup of coffee but serves it extremely hot; there is no savoring. You have to swallow fast, but the aftertaste can't be beat. What are your thoughts? You interested in the job?" It was as though the man was looking straight into his soul. *There ain't much there, padna, and what is there only Trinity can expose; at least, the original version.* There was no doubt Antoine knew the kind of man Babe was, maybe not to the extent of his calling, but he knew he could be brutal when necessary without flinching.

Babe could outstare and outstill anyone. Antoine shifted positions and glanced at a paper he had on his desk. "Yes, sir, I'll do it, but my thoughts, are you certain you want to know?" the older man nodded. "Zama Sakonde is probably dead, or they're holding him as a negotiating chip, and then they'll kill him, and then there's the language barrier. Will I have a contact there? I know most places worldwide understand and speak English, but many times allude to ignorance." Babe tilted his head one way and then the other. The popping of his cervical vertebrae was audible. Antoine's brows arched in surprise. Babe could feel the familiar electricity he'd felt before many of his missions. There was a longing, yet a fear he'd never had, catching his breath and tensing his muscles. Who would be there to protect Chancée? It was his to do.

"Yes. You'll have a contact and have an associate equal to you, but he knows the language." He scribbled something on the paper.

"His name doesn't happen to be Noir?" Babe chuckled. *Wouldn't that beat all?*

With a look of confusion, Antoine answered. "No. I'll call later tonight or when you bring Trinity home, that is, if she's coming home." *Good question,* Babe thought. *Maybe I'll keep ma girl there and play all night.* "When you're back at the house, I'll have all the contact information for you. Do we have an agreement?"

While Babe met with her dad, Trinity installed the car seat and put all the supplies in his truck. She and Chancée waited in the vehicle. Five minutes later, Babe came out the front door. He had a look of fear or concern with a wrinkled forehead, and his eyes seemed to dart all over; then he spied her in his truck.

"Girl, you scared the crap outta me. I would have brought everything from the house. Jesus!" He glanced in the back seat; Chancée was wide awake and silent. "Sweet baby girl, you look beautiful. Daddy's gonna take you home." *Daddy, Dad, Da, Poppa, Pops, no, I'm Daddy,* he decided as all the possibilities ran through his head.

As he slid in the truck, she commented, "So easy for you, but, OMG, I forgot how high this motherfucker was, but I managed. For you it's perfect. Well, Babe, ready to go home?" She came across the same as she did before the tragedy. She talked non-stop from Lake Vista to Chestnut. She excitedly exclaimed as they pulled into the driveway, "The house is gorgeous; what can I say? This is our house?" Gunner was in the backyard and nearly jumped the fence when he saw Trinity. "Shit, he's huge. Sweet?" Babe smiled. He had questions; she was like herself but with a mouth belonging to a Marine. Not that she didn't swear, but not every other word, especially the MF-er.

"Warning: Ruthie doesn't like cursing and has a money jar for each infringement I put a five in now and then, even though I rarely use colorful language, just like with your parents."

She laughed from her belly, "Don't that beat all I can't motherfuck in my own house. Fucking Hell. Do you think I'm that uncouth? Like, 'it's not like I'm gonna hump you at the altar.'" His mouth fell open with surprise.

Sliding out of the car, he started unpacking all the baby things, "For all of the memories we've made, that is the shit you remember?" *Would that have been something the sisters would have shared? Just what had Trinity divulged to Bethany since they became an item?*

Trinity stood on the sideboard, pressed the release button, and grabbed the carrier. Chancée hadn't made a peep the entire ride, but she was open-eyed, taking it all in. "Vic, I think you should carry her, and I'll take some of the baby stuff. I'm scared the dog might knock me down." She brought the carrier to him. "Switch?"

"Wait." He spoke into the phone. "Call Ruthie." It didn't take but a few rings and she was on. "Can you help us bring the baby stuff in?"

He hadn't finished his sentence; she was out the door and gate. "Give me that baby. Won't you look at Nanny Ruth's beautiful girl? I been dying to hold her. You never get a true look when they are in the nursery. Why, Babe, she looks like you but has tiny features like her mom."

Babe watched her every move; something was definitely different about Trinity, but he couldn't put his finger on it. Gunner was curious about the baby but only sniffed at the carrier as though he knew better than to touch her. He was all over Trinity, sniffing her up a storm. She wasn't as head-over-heels with the dog as usual. He guessed it would take time for everyone to assimilate. Ruthie hardly spoke to her. All the attention was on Chancée. The big guy found it odd that Ruthie hadn't asked Trinity how she felt or anything about new motherhood. It was out of character for the house sergeant.

He led her upstairs, carrying the baby, to show off the beautiful nursery he'd assembled. Tickles bubbled in his stomach as he opened the French doors to the baby's room. "Well, ma girl, what you think?"

"It's perfect. You bought all this? Look, even a pink teddy bear. Vic, you're a softy at heart. You surprise me; I mean, you're all manly man; I can't imagine you with all this ruffly pink stuff. It's gonna be a gas rearing a princess, cause you know Antoine is gonna treat her like royalty, um, because it's a grandchild and mine."

Babe smiled his usual one-sided smile, but his gears were grinding. *Antoine? Since when did she refer to her father by his name? That was well beyond the pale, and things are definitely off.* He didn't say anything but placed Chancée delicately in the crib. Whispering to her, he rattled on expressions of adoration. Plain and simple, he was in love with her. Nothing in the world was more precious. By this time, the old Trinity would have cleared her throat, mentioned his lack of attention to her, or been by his side, oohing and cooing over the baby. Memories of the kitten popped into his mind. The way she suckered for the little feline was crazytown, and that was a fucking cat. This was her child, and to stand there silently was most peculiar. It seemed as though the woman he thought was Trinity was actually an impostor. He could understand if Trinity had a twin, but she didn't. Had his woman changed so much he didn't know her? Her calling her dad Antoine kept rolling through his brain, followed by Ruthie's cold behavior and Gunner's intrigue, like when a new person came around.

Babe stroked Chancée's arm and hand. The baby curled her hand on Babe's finger. He watched as her baby blues drifted without rhyme or reason, which was almost disturbing; eventually, her eyelids closed. For those brief moments, she didn't have control of her eyes; it spooked him enough to ignite fluttering in his heart. "That was fuckin weird; her eyes started moving crazy. Is that normal? She looked possessed."

Trinity looked out of the windows, then glanced back at him. "That's par for the course. Want to take a nap? They say sleep when the baby sleeps, but maybe we can do more than sleep." She puckered her lips and turned into their bedroom, pulled down the bedding, and stripped off her clothes.

He emerged from the doorway, locked their bedroom door to the hall, and took off his clothes. He kneeled between her legs and noticed a small scar on her side. "What happened here?" He traced the remnants of an incision with his finger. "Must be from the hospital because I've never noticed it before, but it looks older. Are you sure you are my wife and not a victim of Invasion of the Bodysnatchers?" He chuckled, but there was an undertone of familiarity in his words. *Is this Trinity, or do I just want to see this person as her?*

"I dunno, and shh. I have other plans than to scour your body for ancient injuries." He complied, even though he was sixty percent sure this wasn't his wife. *Why the charade? Was everyone in on it? Had Bethany coached this person as instructed by Antoine and Antoinette? Should I cool this down and say, 'Not today, ma girl?'*

A few hours passed, and it was getting time to feed the baby. He had catnapped and noticed she didn't coil in next to him but tucked her hands under the pillows and slept on her side. Propped on his elbow, he stroked her hair, parting it from the surgical site. The healing scar looked different from most injuries he'd seen, and he had seen a lot. The pinkness of it was too bright, especially against her caramel-colored skin.

Babe announced he was getting in the shower, and the response was an undemonstrative, ho-hum, okay. He mentioned he might have plans for the shower. She asked, like what? Nope, this impostor was not his wife; if it was, he wasn't interested in her. He didn't like her, not at all. She was beautiful but didn't ooze with sass and sex appeal. His Trinity was always looking for an adventure. Who had set this macabre masquerade in motion, and for what reason? It was confusing as all hell.

ONE TO ANOTHER

*T*wo more weeks flew by, and the only information Babe had received from Antoine was that things would happen any day; it was unnerving. If they genuinely wanted to find this Prime Minister alive, they were taking their sweet ass time. Every minute, every hour, then days and weeks, the poor guy had probably been cut up in pieces and thrown to the wild animals, never to be seen by human eyes again.

While her family kept up the pretense, he became increasingly aware of the differences. If it had been a total personality change, that would be one thing, but this was someone impersonating his beloved and doing a piss-poor job of it. If the stranger posing as Trinity wasn't his wife, who was she, and where'd they find so good a double? The changes in her were odd and had all the earmarks of an impostor, but then she'd do something that was so Trinity; it had to be her. The situation was fucked up six ways to Sunday. Life was confusing; however, one thing was for sure: he loved being a daddy. Chancée was just as in love with Babe as he was with her. She was a daddy's girl through and through. He would sit with his feet on the mattress, knees drawn, and place her on the natural incline of his body. He could talk to her constantly as she made grunts and gurgles.

"Chancée, we have to improve your grunting. You sound too much like me, and that's not a good thing, ma girl." It was as though she stared into the depths of his soul. Since daddy duties had begun, something held the demons at bay. Maybe Chancée, so pure and innocent, was like daylight to a vampire. While he couldn't slay the beasts, his precious girl had managed what he could not. *Okay, so maybe it was the Goodness of God in his tiny treasure.* The demons hadn't corrupted her. Anyone trying to bring the evil on her, he'd fuck up in a big kind of way.

Trinity sashayed into the bedroom. "Boy, you ever gonna put that baby down?" She leaned in and held the baby. "Chancée, you are such a daddy's girl; I guess we'll have to give you a brother so I can have a momma's boy," and she laughed. She tossed the phone to Babe, "My dad for you. I guess your disappearing act is about to begin."

Babe sat upright, stoic, and all business. "Yes, sir?"

"Pack a bag and be at the hotel tonight for six. You ready for this?" He asked, already knowing the answer.

"Yes, sir. See you at eighteen, um, six o'clock." The call ended. "Take Chancée to Ruthie, please. I have to pack; I leave this evening." Her expression changed as sadness painted across her face, and her bottom lip began to quiver. He dug deep in the closet and pulled out his gear. It had seemed forever since he'd lugged the gear that held all necessities. Babe checked the contents; he still had the basics like his canteen, binoculars, lighter, flint, flashlights, rope, extra socks, and eating supplies. He needed to add a first aid kit, bug spray, flares, and more bug spray. He remembered what it was like in the Congo, and while some sights could be beautiful, it was a haven for every irritating bug, poisonous plant, and snake. The wild animals muddled about, picking a fight occasionally, but mostly, it was peaceful, and they observed the intruders.

Trinity came back into the room and locked the door. "Boy, you better do me so hard I'll still be able to feel you a month from now." *Now that sounds like Trinity,* he smiled to himself. "I'm not gonna change these sheets til you come home."

Babe cocked his head, "Girl, that's gross. Skank-nasty." There wasn't a twinkle to indicate she recognized the description she used all the time. Maybe she'd be herself or given up the pretense by the time he returned. Maybe Ruthie might straighten her ass out.

After a quick shower and packing experience, they headed to The Backpacker and the grocery for boxes of energy bars. He picked up a water-purifying bottle and called it a day. The next few hours, they played with the baby, Gunner, and waited for the boys to get home. He knew they'd be upset, but he'd already warned them the day was coming.

Babe hugged each boy tight and told them he'd be home as soon as possible and to behave. It was time to head out with a full meal in his belly and zip locks of trail mix, cookies, and some bark-looking bar, all baked and prepared by Ruthie. Kisses, hugs, and a toss of the ball ended the goodbyes, and he headed to Hotel Noelle. His heart was heavy to leave the baby, the boys, and home, yet he felt a different calmness, complete with a resting pulse of sixty and a relaxed gut, thinking that maybe he could figure out the question of Trinity. He'd seen Marines have total personality changes and knew brain trauma was a beast of uncertainty. He had much to think about. It was easy to say in sickness and in health, but there should be a clause that said unless in the case of brain trauma.

Upon entering the lobby, he saw Antoine talking to a distinguished-looking African American man. The man was equal in height to Babe but more slender, like a runner or basketball player. He walked toward the two men. Antoine greeted him, patted his back, and advised they get to the airport and familiarize themselves on the way. The man wore chinos, a white polo, and a blazer and carried a designer suitcase.

In contrast, Babe wore well-worn jeans, a long-sleeved camo tee, his favorite black leather jacket, puncture-resistant boots, and heavy gear on his back. They appeared polar opposites. The airport shuttle pulled in front of the hotel, and the two climbed in. Babe held out his hand; the man shook it and said, "King Belizaire."

With a snortle, Babe replied, "I'm Babe Vicarelli." The man smiled. "And yes, Babe is my given name."

"As King is mine." Both men smiled. So, the supposed dynamic duo was King and Babe. Both men were of a silent nature, and the chatty driver tried to fill the vehicle, but since neither one engaged besides an occasional "hmm," the driver gave into the silence.

The private security company provided business-class seats to accommodate the size of their contract rescue duo. King pulled up the tray, placed his laptop on it, and began reading instructions for the assignment. "Here, read over."

Babe scanned the instructions and committed the contact names to memory. "What intel do you have on the situation we are walking into? You speak French?" The man answered yes, along with most of the languages of the area. "I suppose I'll be the strategist for the retrieval," Babe replied. The man nodded. "Any other manpower?" Concisely, he responded there was a small squadron at base camp. "They will provide us with firearms since no one made provisions for personal weapons?" Babe questioned.

King reclined in the seat, turned his head toward Babe, and commented. "I see," he raised his eyebrows, "This is your first assignment with WSM?" His accent had a slight South African inflection, but it was the first time he noticed. Until then, he hadn't heard any identifiable accent. "They will provide us with everything we need and will have intel on the general location of our assignment. The retrieval will be complex, and we're going in blind. That's where you come in. I understand you can be a ghost, even at your mass." His facial expressions were animated when he spoke with eyebrow waggles, saucer-like eyes, and peculiar shifts in his lips, almost pantomime-likeness. "You are familiar with the Congo and its dangers?"

One side of Babe's lips turned upwards, his natural crooked smile. "More familiar than I care to be. It's brutal in every way, shape, and form, from the treacherous vegetation with skin-tearing thorns to the creatures camouflaged and stalking. I imagine the tension must be obscene with the political unrest and limitless crime. Even at the best of times, I've dealt with some sick Congolese motherfuckers."

On the final leg of the journey, both grabbed some shut-eye and prepared mentally to enter the belly of the beast. No one cared whether they lived or died. There wasn't one bleeding heart who cared about them in the entire country, and there was no safe refuge; all would require forced submission. There were many scenarios during his time in the Corps that the odds were not in their favor, and it took sheer guts and almost savagery to obtain their goals. Hurley always had his six. The thought of him gut-punched with heavy blows. How had he not heard a cry for help in the Marine's voice? It would haunt him to the day when he met his Maker, and he knew now, for sure, there was a Creator. Whether God still wanted to claim him was another question, but looking at Chancée, there was no doubt. God was real.

The landing was far from smooth as they bounced down the runway of one of the smaller airports. It finally came to a stop. Babe followed King since he knew the WSM protocol. They passed through the airport and met a dark-skinned woman with a red beret and fatigues. They commenced speaking in a language other than French. Babe remembered a minuscule amount of French from college.

Having a decent internal compass, he figured they were farther north than the capital. Glances out the window mainly appeared green, unlike the urban areas he remembered. One mission he recalled took them close to the northern swamp with warnings to beware of gorillas. There was not much about the Congo he found appealing.

The setting and atmosphere created waves of concern. Babe flashed back to the rescue of trafficked victims with Jarvis and his crew, where he felt a sense of belonging and control from the get-go. King and the woman appeared to have zero military experience, and it felt like the woman had picked up a traveling salesman and his trained monkey, referring to himself—a bit unfair, maybe all brawn and no brain. Babe did not like the environment; it felt dishonest, contrived, and fucking dangerous because of the secrecy or deception. There were no other people on the team present. Either they would be on the same page, or the rescue they planned had more holes than working girls' fishnet stockings. Maybe that was the plan. The longer the walk to the car took, the more ill-at-ease he became. He had nothing for protection. All he had was a hidden knife as part of his belt buckle.

"Ma'am, can we stop for a moment? My name is Babe Vicarelli, and you are? Oh, and English would be preferable if we are to get anything close to accomplished. Failed rescues or missions are not part of my repertoire. Either read me in, or I'm on the next flight back to the States."

She turned abruptly and, without a glimmer of pleasantry, replied, "I will read you in when I choose." She stood with shoulders pinned back, a dour expression on her face, and intense scrutiny in her eyes.

Babe shifted his eyes toward King and spoke, "Is this what you call a collaborative effort? Because, chief, if you do, I'm getting the fuck out of here." Babe's body was rigid, and he had a look that screamed it wasn't a threat; it was a fact, no doubt. He started to turn.

The woman spoke; her shoulders had dropped, and the painted face of a control freak had vanished. "I did not intend to insult or keep you in the dark. You are a vital part of the success of this rescue. Please accept my apologies; it is a most serious time here. My name is Valentina Philipe; I am part of the security team for the office of the prime minister." She put her hand out to shake his. He accepted the apology, but in the back of his mind, he thought *somebody screwed the pooch*. King remained silent.

Waiting for them was a car festooned with flags, screaming government dignitary. This was not the suitable transport if they were going for stealth and expected him to be a ghost. Sure as shit, a half mile from the airport, a worn truck and an open off-road vehicle forced them from the well-worn dusty road. The militants held them at gunpoint.

They shot the driver and tore the flags off the car. One person dressed in all black with a face mask covering all but his eyes slid into the driver's seat while another masked person forced their way into the back seat. Babe felt confident he could take the two out, but then he'd have to deal with the people in the other vehicle. Maybe they would bring them to the same place they had held the prime minister, that is, if he wasn't already dead. King spoke to Valentina, but before the man was able to get two words out, the captor slammed the butt of their outdated but effective machine gun into his face, splitting the skin over King's cheekbone and eyebrow. Blood ran onto his pristine white shirt. Valentina screamed and started to say something; Babe held his hand over her mouth and drew her close.

King started to speak again, and the dark-skinned man held up the butt of the gun, threatening to smash him again. It was more than evident to the trained eye that the gunman had limited skills, and based on body size and musculature, Babe figured he was young, twenty at most, and more like a teen. If all their soldiers were as green, he could take them down, but that was a huge if. If it were his operation, everyone would be highly skilled and trained, but if there were no other option, send one skilled and one novice with limited skills and keep the brass away from the fray. Someone in the prime minister's office or even the Presidential office leaked their arrival. The attack was too organized to be a coincidence, considering their seeming lack of experience.

The yahoos in the open-off-road vehicle started shooting their guns in the air. An accomplished warrior could easily take down such bravado bullshit. It seemed like an amateur hour or a night of carousing with the boys. Why had Antoine given him the idea that his two-man team were of like mind and skill? Another Noelle mystery or game. He didn't get it; to Babe, it was a mystery. King showed no sign of military skill. Maybe he was putting on a pretense until they got where they were going. One school of thought was he planned the sabotage so the captors would take them to the hide-out and perhaps the prime minister. Things were convoluted and fucked up beyond all recognition in the U.S., but the Congo made the deception of the States look like tomfoolery. He vividly remembered a conversation with a commanding officer warning him there was not one trustworthy inhabitant of the Congo—to be ready to fight for survival at all times. It wasn't just the people, but the terrain was inhospitable. Danger or death may be lurking at every turn.

In some ways, it was inexperience on the part of the captors because they neither blindfolded nor placed a hood over the three of their heads. Babe counted the clicks and sketched the route they drove in his mind: definitely north, away from any perception of civilization. *Fairly simple*. Valentina wiggled her way from Babe's grasp, but he knew she was thankful or she'd gotten cracked or shot, being a woman. He hoped they didn't separate them, or the captors would probably have their way and then kill her for pleasure when they finished playing with the new toy.

A plume of dust exploded as the vehicle in front of them abruptly stopped. The tiny encampment consisted of four small shanty shacks. *I hope our base camp has more teeth*, he thought; *if not, we're fucked*. A strong gale wind would wipe out the matchstick huts. Two men from the open air off-road joined their escort and pointed their weapons at them while shouting unintelligible words, even to the ears of those who spoke their language. They signaled with the barrels of their guns, forcing the prisoners to walk toward the largest of the shacks. Getting closer, Babe reckoned they weren't as flimsy as first thought but something he could muscle his way through if need be. Certainly, the walls were no protection from actual gunfire, maybe a twenty-two, pellet gun, or slingshot, but that would be it. Anything with more umph would slice the walls like a hot knife through butter.

As though bad to the bone with a major attitude, the captors shoved King and Valentina to the ground and pointed a gun for Babe to sit. The smaller captor flung a knife from his pocket, catching Babe with a slight scratch, but tore his shirt to shit. The more experienced soldier garbled something to the one Babe pegged as a boy, and the boy jumped, grabbed twine, and wrapped it a few times around Babe's wrists, waist, and legs, then knotted it. *This is almost comedic. One flex and the restraints are gonna pop like Mardi Gras beads.* Perhaps because King dressed like he was attending a social gathering at the club, they assumed he had no military training. To Babe, he would agree, but somewhere inside said WSM purposefully had him cast in that role, and when the time came, he'd show a warrior mentality, at least he hoped. The captors left the boy in charge of watching the prisoners while they reported to their superiors or prepared for their execution.

The boy cursed at them and kicked dirt in Babe's direction. The big man stared straight at the kid with a look that would have shaken the devil himself—an intense, blank expression with no hint of humanity. The youngster commented they didn't scare him and could kill them at any time. Babe glared with emptiness.

Thirty minutes passed, and he heard footsteps heading toward them. Junior, the name Babe tagged the boy with, jumped to attention as the door opened. If he didn't know better, he would have sworn the general, or at least he looked like the man in charge, was Samuel L. Jackson; if not, a stunt double. He spoke clear and articulate English.

"Sir," looking at King, "What is your purpose for coming to the Congo, especially during this time of unrest? Do you not know it is a most dangerous proposition?" King's face was a mess, with his eye swollen shut from the combination of the gash above his eye and the cheekbone below. "I see my men made an impression on you. Smooth talking will not get you in a better position." He glared down at King. Speaking to another one of his associates in his native language, Babe figured he told the man to take the woman because she shrieked with terror.

Babe was on the brink of saying 'not on his watch' when King replied that she was an important person and could be used as a bargaining chip if left alone, but if harm or violation occurred, it would bring the wrath of the President. He made a broad declaration that his company was scouting areas for development; hence, his company's executives had reached out to a branch of their government. King wasn't concerned with their political issues; he was just making a fortune for himself and everyone involved. The general's eyes flickered when he heard the word fortune. Greed was a powerful motivator, despite the efforts they were supposedly making against Westernization. In one fell swoop, King had lowered the guard of the soldiers. *Maybe that's what he brings to the table—he's a bullshit artist.*

As far as Babe was concerned, the name of the game was finding the prime minister. Did the Congolese trolls have him in camp, or had they executed him? Babe could easily see why they wanted to keep the pristine areas of their country free of the pollution of the Western world; at least seventy or eighty percent had already become urbanized while they raped the land of its resources; oil and minerals.

The two men spoke with an occasional chuckle. Then, the general pointed to Babe. He guessed, figuring out where he played into the picture. "General Penaile, this is Vic; our company sent him as a safety measure." The man laughed, reflecting that one man could hardly provide protection from his militia, albeit small. Babe couldn't help but think, *give me five minutes and see who comes out on top.* He needed to focus on the main objective, the Prime Minister.

King produced a flask from his pocket, took a swig, and offered it to Penaile. *Good, get him sauced, loosen his lips, and slow his reaction time.* They didn't bother to offer a taste to the woman or Babe. After half an hour, the two men were depleting the flask, but Penaile left and returned with a bottle and two cigars. Indicating he needed a piss, Babe was allowed to leave the hut. He went behind one of the primitive buildings, unescorted, to his amazement, and skirted the periphery. Unfortunately, there weren't signs of a captured Prime Minister. Strike two, figuring strike one was their party of three being held captive. Babe returned to the hut after checking the area so as not to raise suspicions. Why they let him go alone was a mystery, but the whole thing was convoluted, piss-poor planning, and amateur hour. Babe ripped the rest of his shirt off and shoved it in his pocket.

The sun was beginning to lower in the sky. The general flicked his head to the side, indicating they were to follow. He took King in his vehicle, and everyone else went in another. The road was make-shift as they banged and bumped through the terrain, coming to another encampment with far more civilized buildings and double the number of soldiers. The foliage surrounding the camp was thick, creating a canopy overhead. Those flying over would have a difficult time seeing them. The younger men nudged Babe and Valentina with the muzzle of their weapons into a building different from King's, who appeared chummy with the general.

One of the boys spoke a little English. Babe asked for his bag. They had already gone through it and taken whatever they wanted, leaving most of his things intact. Knowing there was no harm, the boy went to the vehicle and returned with Babe's gear. He pulled out the granola bars, offering one to the woman and the boys. No takers. The captors had already consumed Ruthie's other tasty tidbits. The granola bars must not have been to their liking because only one was missing. In the distance, he heard the unmistakable sound of gunfire. The soldiers jumped toward the door. A few old, dinged-up trucks pulled into the area, followed by a black dignitary car. Babe spied the President exit the long vehicle. Pulling the hidden knife from his belt, he torqued the neck of one soldier, and before the other soldier realized, Babe slit the neck of the other in a flash. He grabbed Valentina's hand. They slipped into the darkness of the night.

Now that Babe had a more precise understanding that all was rotten in the Congo, it was each man for themselves. Dollars to donuts, the Prime Minister was either held captive or hiding somewhere of his own volition, perhaps in the building they brought King into. They made tracks as they hauled ass through the thick vegetation, maybe with a half-hour or twenty-minute headstart. Babe set his sights on returning to the landing strip and either paying or highjacking an exit to the States. The whole thing smelled of bullshit; whether it was Antoine's made-up crap or King's was up for debate. After this debacle, he decided to work with Jarvis in between taking care of Trinity, the boys, and Chancée. Babe was glad he'd never shared his address with Antoine. He could use some Javier intel at this point, but Javier wouldn't necessarily know of the dealings in the Congo. Still, the cartel kingpin had surprised Babe in too many situations, and he knew anything was possible.

They wove through the thick jungle that seemed to edge the makeshift road. Rough, dinged-up trucks and old, dented vehicles sped down the road. "Keep low. If you want to turn back, you can, but I'm getting as far from this fucked situation as possible. Your choice." When the boy soldiers had gone through his things, they'd put his phone back in the bag, maybe because it was an old model with a cracked screen. Service was non-existent or spotty at best. Every few miles, he'd check again. Finally, he had bars and punched in a familiar number. "How are you, Marine?"

"Gotta get out of the Congo." He heard a loud exhalation of aggravation.

"What the fuck? The Congo, are you mad? On Uncle Sam's dime?"

Babe was crouched low. Valentina constantly complained, which was enough to send him around the twist. "Long story. It's safe to say things are not as they seem. Can you or not?"

There was a silence of deliberation. "Yes, but it'll be at a cost. Nothing is free." Babe could hear Javier pace; he could visualize Casa Garcia, the expansive house with wings designed like the spokes of a bicycle.

Another vehicle approached, this time at a terrific speed. The rebel Congolese found their dead compadres and high-tailed it after their prisoners, more for the woman than him. "I have a woman with me."

"Extra weight." Point blank, no bargaining. "Move it, Marine; she'll only slow you down." *Agreed.* They arranged a location close to the coast. It would take him a couple of days to get there if all went without complications, but they conspired a plan.

"Valentina, are you familiar?" He swept his hand, indicating the area. She nodded. "Are you close to a safe place?" She shrugged one shoulder.

"I didn't get where I am by being a fraught chambermaid. I'm close enough to protection. I heard you talk of the sea. It's a long distance but make your way west. Remember, cowboy, you have no friends here."

They continued, concealed by dense foliage, and advanced in the dusky hours and through the night. They both had cuts and abrasions from the vegetation. Under a full moon, she stopped him and said that was where they'd go their separate ways.

Once unencumbered by the woman, Babe made tracks fast, hiding in cargo trucks, all heading west.

THIS FOR THAT

*J*avier had been true to his word. As the ocean came into view on the very edge of the horizon, Babe watched the helicopter hover above the coastline. He took off running when someone let down a cable from the bird, and, like so many other times, hand over hand, he scaled into the helo as it lifted him in. The pilot wasted no time and banked into the open blue skies.

To his surprise, Javier was along for the ride, "Marine, you never change. What kind of mischief have you gotten yourself into?" It was unfortunate for Babe that his one and only friend was a cartel boss. Their interaction was like two friends; seeing his smile felt good. "We must stop meeting like this, or my wife will grow jealous. And what is it with no shirt? What, you are a Chip and Dale dancer?" The big man chuckled.

Babe commented he'd unwind the story over a couple of Glenlivet tumblers, and no, he wasn't a Chippendale dancer. One of the captors sliced through his shirt, catching his neck, and tossed his shredded garment at him. He rested, watching the scenery change, and he could see nothing but water. After an hour, the pilot landed on one of the biggest private yachts he'd ever seen. Javier led the way to the main living or partying space. A young man approached him with a two-finger pour of Glenlivet. Babe glanced at Javier and raised his glass. The amenities exuded wealth and power. Javier's wife, Maria, and her sister, Carmen, approached from a doorway with warm, long-time friend hugs. His thoughts cast back to his and Carmen's interlude. It had wreaked havoc in his heart and twisted the screwdriver of guilt in his belly.

Since the change in the complexion of his marriage, he welcomed Carmen's attention and considered the possibilities. No doubt he was gonna tap that if offered. After winding down a bit, Javier led Babe to the guest quarters, complete with an on-suite bath. Babe had a change of clothes in his gear, but Javi had already instructed one of the crew to arrange casual boating attire folded on the bed. Javi grabbed Babe's arm, "I know how much you loved Trinity; I was heartsick when I heard of her passing." Without exhibiting emotion, Babe nodded as his heart crushed. *Dead. How, when?* "Shower and join me upstairs." The words tumbled in his mind over and over. *Dead?*

He stood in the shower and let the spray of water tickle his back. Not only did he have much to tell his friend, but evidently, his friend had much to tell him. Barefooted, in jeans and a tee with a tumbler in his hand, Babe climbed the stairs; the boating attire was not his style. He sat on what he imagined a casting couch looked like. How much pleasure took place right where he was sitting. The same young man brought a tray of fruit, rolled meat, cheeses, a large bowl of chips, and a green dip. Babe chowed down. Once he gathered his thoughts, he began questioning Javi, which he surmised was not part of the plan. Javi smiled.

"Javier, when I left New Orleans, Trinity was home with Chancée, so forgive my curiosity. You said dead?" Try as he did, he knew his face reflected fear.

"You mean when you left Angelette le Bateau, not Trinity, my friend. Surely, there had to be intimate differences." Javier swiveled in the captain's chair and asked the boy to bring two more drinks. "I know the women are uncannily similar, but it's hardly surprising, being that Antoinette and her sister Jeanette are flawlessly identical, and her husband is a distant relative to Antoine. Those genes are strong. I think they pulled the ruse in fear of losing contact with the child, not as an offense to you. That's all they'll have left of their daughter."

Babe shook his head and drained the second drink in one swallow, asking for a third. "As if I'd do that. Fuck, Trinity is dead?" He could feel the tears fill his eyes, a lump develop in his throat, and the crush of heartbreak.

"From what I heard, she was holding on by a thread and lost in a dark sea of uncertainty—poor girl. My sources say the family refers to her in the past tense, implying her death. I shouldn't have referred to her as dead. I am sorry, my friend." Rolling through Babe's mind were all the minor differences he'd noticed. Checking himself, he knew the woman claiming to be Trinity wasn't his wife, but he wanted it so desperately he played in the duplicity. Who knew? How many were in on the game? How the fuck did Javier know? The whole thing was a mind fuck. He still couldn't believe that Antoinette and Antoine would create such a lie. Did they really think he'd keep the baby from them?

Babe pressed the heel of his hand against his forehead. The emotional games were too much to take in. "Do you know where she is? Who knows about their deception?" He cleared his throat, trying to force the anxious bile down. Babe swirled the amber liquid around the third glass as though the answer would magically appear like a crystal ball. "I want to see her." The thought of knocking boots with Carmen had all but vanished. The lie and the whys were his main focus.

"I will try to find out for you. Remember I told you my help came at a cost? One day, I'll collect, but right now, I'll get you to New Orleans. You'll owe me one." Javier sucked the last mouthful of his drink through his teeth.

After a few days at sea, they anchored just off Cartagena. The crew lowered a smaller boat into the water, and Javier, Maria, Carmen, two bodyguards, and Babe boarded. They sped off like a racehorse out the gate or the proverbial bat out of Hell. It had been an intriguing time. Javier and Babe gathered in Javi's private office. They talked about the world, the mess in America, the dangers in Colombia, and how different things had been since they were kids, even though Javier was older and his youth had been significantly different. Still, the world seemed stable for years. One could have easily lost sight that it was a serial killer and cartel boss bouncing ideas around and not just any two guys passing the time. Carmen had politely flirted but observed the wedding ring on Babe's finger. She and Maria had questions about the baby and carried on like hens, the way many women behave with the talk of children.

Babe noticed Javier was edgier than usual and not in his nonchalant, sophisticated way. His eyes darted, and his movements were manic. He was distracted. The Marine leaned forward. "You're pensive. What's got under your skin? Where's the suave, sophisticated Bossman?" Javier glanced off into the distance, obviously with a head full of thoughts. No, he no longer seemed cold and calculating, the controller of his destiny. There was an air of trepidation and heightened alert.

Javier plucked a piece of lime wedged on the rim of his glass and bit into it. Just the thought set Babe's teeth on edge. He explained that there had been two intense attempts on his life and a few break-ins at Casa Garcia. He surmised one of his people had turned, but he was lost as most of his crew had been with him for years, a few from childhood. Babe got pissed and concerned for the cartel boss causing his gut to fall, creating a wake of stress tagged with a curdling of acid, which bubbled geysers exploding from his stomach. He wanted to offer his assistance but needed to get back to the States. His mind circled the possibilities of conversations with Antoine and Antoinette. Checking himself, he'd stick true to character and boldly confront them with the new-found knowledge. It was incomprehensible that they would fabricate such a story. "Come home with me, Javi. Once I put the problem in New Orleans to rest, I will be your bodyguard until I find the traitor, and either you or I can exact their punishment. You will be safe at my home. It's a haven for wayward boys," and he chuckled with a wink. "Nobody knows of it. Your wife and sister-in-law are welcome as well."

"And what of our children?" Javier raised his eyebrows as though putting up an obstacle to Babe's solution. "I might have accepted the invitation, but I am moving my family to Barcelona. My home there, like yours, is under the radar. We will leave for New Orleans in the morning, and I will be your bodyguard." Javier laughed.

"Padre, I don't need a fuckin bodyguard. Right now, I have done nothing wrong; believe me, I will get to the bottom of this. Oh, Antoine doesn't like strangers."

"Neither do I." The two men touched glasses, welcoming a film coating of the libations down their throats. On the way to his room, Babe stopped by the kitchen for an orange and took Carmen's hand, leading her to his quarters. Carmen willingly followed. Once the door closed, he pushed her against the door with a hard, deep kiss, caressing her breasts. He lifted her casual dress over her hips, then freed himself. There was no emotion, merely release.

It hadn't been Trinity who'd betrayed him, but he was still piping angry about the ruse. His interlude with Carmen quenched his need for a physical connection. She was more than beautiful with soft, sultry red lips, curves in all the right places, and a willingness to please. Javier knew Carmen had a fascination with the Marine. If it were true that his woman was dead, perhaps he might explore another wife, maybe to bear him more children. Even knowing what she did about Babe, his propensity for violence, and similar ways to Javier, who could be ruthless, she saw a quiet, gentle way about him, which intrigued her. The brutal killer lay buried beneath layers of silence. She made herself at his beck and call, playing the dutiful wife. The fantasy of a life with the military man grew like a young girl with a crush. Javier and Maria had kept her from situations where she might meet possible suitors for safety and overall security. The men of Casa Garcia feared for their lives if they approached her or made any untoward advances, but she could see how they desired her. She felt cloistered like a

THE IMPOSTOR LIE

nun. Carmen fantasized about being swept away to the United States by the American.

Babe basked in the silence of the night. Wrong or right, the soft purs from the woman beside him brought memories with Trinity. His tiny woman would curl into him, tucking her body as close as possible. Carmen sculpted her body next to his, like spoons in a drawer. Her skin was soft and velvety. While his Trinity was the hottest thing on two legs, part of her intrigue was her flippant personality, which made her always ready for a toe-to-toe. While exotically exquisite, Carmen was too malleable, exhibiting zero intestinal fortitude. Her opinions seemed shallow and borderline non-existent. She was excellent wife material for the man who wanted a clean house, ironed shirts, dinner at six, and a tumble on command. That didn't do it for Babe. He needed a woman to fight him, stand up to him, question his decision, and slay him in the boudoir with demands. How could he tell Carmen that their tryst was nothing more than just that and her fantasies of being his little woman were a pipedream? Fucking her was slightly better than a lathered jerk-off. The thought made him feel guilty. She wanted more, yet while checking boxes to satisfy most men, he needed something unlike most because he was far different than the average Joe.

He stared at the ceiling as the feelings of guilt traversed his mind. Quietly, Carmen awoke and watched him. She ran her hands down his body, tickling with her delicate touch. He put his hand on top of hers to stop the inevitable. Propping on her elbow, she gazed at him while he bore holes of ideas in the ceiling. "Sir, is something wrong? Do you not desire me?"

"Carmen, it's not you; it's me. You are beautiful and kind. Any man would be flattered to share a bed with you. My mind is on pressing issues. I'd like nothing more than a roll with you, but matters require my attention." He moved his hand, and she continued down the happy trail. "Do not be gentle with me. I need you to take charge of my body aggressively. Draw me from my thoughts." As per his request, she punished his body, biting his muscular chest. She tightened her grip and performed bordering on painful control. He moaned aloud and flipped her onto her back, drilling her with pounding thrusts. She fed the primal beast in him. Their bodies glistened with sweat.

"Is that how you like it?" She asked. He smiled with his one-sided grin. She whispered, "I am happy I pleased you. Do you want me to slap you or talk sexy?" He closed his eyes and shook his head.

"You always please; it's just that sometimes I need more. There is nothing wrong with you. The complexities are mine." He saw the need to please him in her eyes. If anything, other than beautiful, she was built to please. "I think I will leave for the States with Javier in the morning, but I will be back."

After a thorough workout the following morning, he showered and ate, and the men left for the airport, leaving Casa Garcia's lush paradise behind. The lives they led were vastly different from any usual standard. Babe wanted what the rest of the population had: a life of certainty, no guesswork or life-threatening drama. He welcomed the typical saying of 'same old, same old.'

Once in the air, the discussion began about how he should handle Antoine and Antoinette. If, in fact, Trinity was holding on by a thread, he wanted to be by her side when she took her last breath. She was his everything, and now that he knew he wasn't losing his shit and the woman at his house, indeed, was an impostor, he could bow out of the game and find his love. While many people might be afraid of standing up to Antoine, Babe hadn't met anyone he was scared to challenge except Trinity before the beating, but that was part of their game. No doubt, she could slay him with a look. He loved the girl from the deepest part of his being.

The only person outside of Trinity that he could call a friend was the head of a powerful cartel, proof enough that he'd stand up to anyone. He remembered holding a knife at Javier's throat. Crossing Babe's mind was perhaps he wanted someone to take him out. He'd long passed swallowing his gun; for some strange reason, he couldn't do it, but he was more than willing to leverage his life over and over without fear. Was he hoping someone would snuff him? He remembered someone told him that the most dangerous opponent was the one that had nothing to lose. Maybe he was that man, but now, he had to consider Chancée. She was young enough to forget all about him if he crossed the line and bit it.

Was his mission still to right wrongs and fight for those who couldn't? Would Trinity still consider him a superhero? Was he still the same man in the mirror?

Javier sipped on his water with a contemplative look. "Marine, you haven't said one word and have that light on, but nobody home stare. What are you so heady about?" He crossed his legs and turned in the chair, looking directly at Babe, who looked back with a half smile. "Are you hung up on talking to Antoine? You've never been scared," he fashioned air quotations, "to approach me. I think the man is tame compared to me." Javier's brow furrowed. His Marine friend was a complicated man, yet primal to the core.

"The thing is, I want to see Trinity. Sure, I could hold him at gunpoint and demand to see her, but that's not the direction I want this to go. My life finally seemed to settle; I had sort of a family with them. If she is on death's doorstep, I want to be with her to the end—Not forgetting to mention why they created a ruse in the first place. The whole thing is fuckin bizarre. They did a similar thing when Chance was on the verge of death; they fed hope to Trinity that he might get better. Is it because her parents can't handle delivering such news that they create their own narrative or deceptive game? I'm new to this whole family dynamic thing, but I know I don't pull punches with the boys. Those little fuckers know they can depend on what I say. I'm no fucking bullshitter."

Javier stood, poured a Glenlivet shot, and then handed it to Babe, who didn't think twice and tossed the liquid down his throat. He started up again, "And then what the fuck was this WSM mission? That's why I was in the Congo—some other stupid charade. Supposedly, the loyalists abducted the Prime Minister in protest of the changes they wanted to bring into the country. It was all civil issues, and I was to ghost him out as part of a contract team of professionals. Fuck me; they picked us up from the airport in some dignitary vehicles with fucking flags. Imbeciles." He shook his head with eyes closed tightly. His next thought was what he wouldn't have given for his heavyweight bag. His muscles twitched with the need to hurt someone, and his best solution for his aggression was the heavyweight bag.

The two sat in silence for the next ten minutes, then Javier broke the stifled air. "I don't know why they played those foolish games, Marine, but I know; I don't tell my wife about anything but rainbows and unicorns. What a strange expression you Americans have created to describe a carefree existence. I say, be gracious and polite but direct and call them out on the girl, Angelette. They'll take you to Trinity, wherever she may be. Now relax or talk to yourself. I need to take care of some business." As though a thought popped into his mind, he asked Babe, "You like Carmen? Also, Amigo, I know of this contract company you speak of, and they usually kick ass, but they are American owned, so I guess they, too, play games." He opened his laptop and glanced at the big man, "The offer to work with me is a standing offer. Be my bodyguard, and you will make more money than you can spend."

Babe stood, walked to the bottle of whiskey, and poured more into his glass. "I'll keep it under advisement." Feeling a slight warmth in his gut, Babe could turn off the messages in his brain and relax, looking at the big blue sky. He reflected on Javi's offer, but he had responsibilities with the house, the boys, Chancée, and sorting through the mess with Angelette, the fake Trinity. Babe let his mind wander back to amusing times at Louie's. Since the beating, he wondered if he'd ever find Louie's entertaining or a place for respite again. His heart ached for his little woman, and it punched his gut like a champion world-class boxer.

Once at the airport, they hailed a cab and went straight to Chestnut. Ruthie was delighted Babe was home, and he saw a glimmer in her eyes when she met Javier. His Colombian friend could be so suave with the women, and he laid it on with the house commander. Babe swore he could see a slight glow on her face, like a young girl.

She graciously showed Javier to a guest room and placed towels on his bed. "Thank you, Miss Ruthie. Bonita."

Babe walked down the hall to his bedroom. The fake Trinity was reading a magazine on the bed. "Back already? That was a quick trip, not even a week. Glad you're here." She started to get up.

"Read your magazine, Angelette. I want to see my baby girl." He continued into the nursery.

The girl began sputtering, "B-but, h-how?" He obviously took her off-guard. "Look, I was going to tell you. I knew you could tell I wasn't Trinity." She pulled at the long hair, and half of it came off. The hair left, her hair, was almost shoulder length, and the unnatural, weird-looking plastic scar came off with the long fake hair. She appeared older than Trinity, but their likeness was uncanny. "Sorry for the deception. My mother and Antoinette used to fool people since they were twins. They thought it might work with me and T." She looked at the floor with shame. "It wasn't my idea."

Babe held Chancée and towered over the little woman. "Where is my wife? I need to see her now! Get your stuff and get me to her." He turned and looked at her and said disgustedly, "And you even seduced me to the bed. I felt guilty and uneasy since the memory loss; I said as much. I guess I should have paid you; that's what one does with working girls."

The girl jerked around, eyes squinted, and retorted with venom, "How dare you disrespect me like that."

"Disrespect you? You must be fuckin crazy. You were a part of the deception, and I almost bought into it because of my distraught. Fuck you." Then, he carried his princess into the guest room. "Javier, meet my daughter, Chancée." Still, with a calm demeanor, she quietly gazed at her daddy. "This is my girl." He kissed the top of her head. Angelette followed into the room, saying she was ready to go.

"Marine, she is muy hermoso; the young bucks will be lining up at your door. Keep working the weights; scare the crap out of them. She has blue eyes like you. You have yourself one beautiful white girl." He pointed to the door with a flick of his head. "Go see your wife; I'll visit with Miss Ruthie downstairs and wait for your boys to get home." He peered around Babe, "Hello, Angelette. You fucked with the wrong Marine. You're fortunate he didn't put you down like a dog. I don't get the American games." Then, Babe noticed her eyes were golden, not the ebony of Trinity's, answering why her eyes looked odd. She had worn colored contacts.

Babe wanted to knock the shit out of her and give the Noelle's a piece of his mind, but a cooler head prevailed. They had had their share and then some of tragedy and death. Perhaps that offset their unreasonable action; as long as he saw Trinity, that was all that mattered. The more he looked at the girl, the more he became perplexed regarding their game. How could he have been so blind? His eye for detection failed miserably. Was he looking with hope? She wasn't sassy or energetic, of course; she had sustained a brain injury, he told himself, which could have been explanation enough, but what about the scar on her abdomen? That, in itself, should have been enough to call everyone out. It was funny how hope could paint a picture.

Once in the living room, Ruthie commented with a hand on her hip, "Well, it's about time the truth came out. You might be kin to Miss Trinity, but you sure ain't her. Our girl has genteel ways—shame on you, and shame on whoever put you up to this charade. You ain't fooled anyone except Babe, and it was because he wanted to believe." The girl eyed her, looking like she wanted to say something, but there wasn't anything to say.

Babe addressed Ruthie, "Ma'am, with Angelette's help, I'm going to see my wife. Javier will hang here with you and Gunn if you don't mind." Her lips turned into a smile like a bow. No, she not only didn't mind, but she was thrilled. "You'll keep an eye on this one?" He handed her Chancée.

Angelette climbed into Babe's truck. When they pulled off, she explained that she was sorry and that it wasn't her fault. A pressured squeeze grew in his chest. He wanted to know who knew and if she had seen Trinity. The picture in his mind was like a rolling film of possibilities for Trinity's appearance. "T. looks like she's sleeping with a few tubes in her body, at least when I saw her last. Nobody thinks she'll make it, but she's stronger than her family gives her credit." She drummed her fingers on the door armrest. The facility was a three-story building on St. Charles Avenue. They pulled alongside and parked.

Babe started to slide out. "Lock yourself in, and I'll be back in about an hour." His face etched with determination was a scary prospect. She grabbed his sleeve and told him they wouldn't let him in; she had to go with him. She clarified that she knew he wanted to be alone with his wife. Babe shrugged a shoulder and agreed, thinking whatever it took to get inside.

The security guard, a man in his early fifties with a belly draping his belt, acknowledged Angelette. He said Mr. and Mrs. Noelle were in her room. *Well, two birds with one stone.* They had some explaining to do, and it better not wreak of bullshit. He felt a slow boil begin in his gut. The flushing made its way up, and the veins in his neck pulsed. Anyone could see the anger and know they better get out of his way.

They got off the elevator on the second floor. Angelette timidly spoke. "There's only one other patient besides T. Do you want me to ask my aunt and uncle to step out?" Her voice was jittery from nerves. She had failed at the impersonation and alienated him. It was a lose-lose situation for her. What could she say to them? Babe closed his eyes and shook his head. *Fuck no*, he thought, *catch 'em by surprise.*

Babe pushed the door open. The expression on her parents' faces was surprise and fear wrapped into one. Mama Noelle came from the far side of the bed. "It's good to see you, honey." *Really,* he thought.

"Is it now? I have a truckload of questions for y'all, but first, I want to spend time with my wife. Could you give me some time alone with her?" With a series of affirmations, she left the room. Antoine quietly asked how things went with WSM. "It was a shit show. I don't know if they didn't give it to you straight or you didn't level with me, but whatever, it was an unplanned disaster that could have gotten people killed unnecessarily. I'm one and done with them." Antoine apologized and said they'd talk later. "For sure," Babe replied with a stern, no-nonsense intonation in his voice.

He pulled a chair close to the bed and held her hand. She was down to skin and bones, with a frail look to her appearance. Babe's stomach knotted and chest tightened as he tried to swallow the lump that gave him a stranglehold. *Pull it together*, he said to himself. He kissed her hand.

"Trinity, it's Babe. I miss you insanely. You have to get well to care for our beautiful daughter, Chancée. She's got your happy-go-lucky personality, but my blue eyes. We have a pale girl, like my mother; hopefully, her pigment will get darker with time, just like yours. I've researched brain trauma and comas, so I'm going to try the suggestions." He cleared his throat, waiting nervously until his heart settled, then began. "Trinity, if you're inside, squeeze my hand." Nothing. A single tear rolled down his cheek. It might have been his imagination, but suddenly, he felt a slight pressure on his hand. *Probably wishful thinking.* "Trinity, if you can feel my hand, squeeze mine." The response was much quicker, and he felt pressure. His heart pounded, and he felt like he could hardly breathe. The tears trickled down his face. "My sassy girl, this means you can get better; we just have to give it time."

A physical therapist knocked and entered. "So sorry, sir. I didn't—"

"Do what you need to do for my wife." She began talking to Trinity as she exposed one of her lifeless legs, which looked like a matchstick. Looking at her state of wellness screamed they had years until she would be better, if ever. "Ma'am, I asked her to squeeze my hand if she was inside her body, and I felt a soft, almost absent pressure against my hand. Could it be?" His eyes were full of hope and longing.

"Trinity, did you try to hold your man's hand? We got to move these legs; you don't want contractures, girl. As it is, your dancer legs look more like a stick person. I hear you rock, so we gotta keep your legs movin', sweetie." She raised a shoulder, looking at Babe, "It's possible, but I haven't seen any sign. It might be an involuntary twitch." Babe told her to hold Trinity's hand gently, and then he spoke, telling her it was him and to squeeze his hand again if she could. The therapist's eyes popped wide open, and an ear-to-ear smile painted her face. "Now, Trinity, you been holding out until your man got here? I expect to see you daily if this is the progress you incite, Mister. You her husband?" She glanced in his direction, and he nodded. "We're gonna start trying harder to wake you, so prepare yourself for more rigorous activity." She winked at Babe. PT lasted for another half an hour. "Sir, I'll see you tomorrow. Let her rest." Babe inquired if he could bring the baby to lay on her chest. "I'll talk to the doctor, but probably not. Not yet, at least."

"Yes, ma'am." He continued to hold her hand as the therapist left the room. "Now I know you're in there, and there is much to tell you. I miss you, girl. I'm sorry I wasn't there to protect you; I failed you. Your cousin Angelette pretended to be you, and I don't know if it was just wishful thinking on my part but I believed it, sort of. She coaxed me into bed, although it didn't take much; I suspected it wasn't you, but head trauma can change people. There was no fire. The way you turn me on is different than anything else in the world. Maybe you'll get mad enough and wake to beat the snot out of her." He thought he detected a hint of a twitch of her lips, and her heart rate accelerated. He knew for sure she could hear him. "I don't know who the instigator of the charade was, but I will get to the bottom of it. You can count on that, sexy lady." Her heart rate settled down to normal. "Now that I know where they've stashed you, I'll be that pain in your ass who harasses you. You'll want to wake up and say, 'Boy, would you shut the fuck up?' We're gonna get you better every day." He kissed her forehead, then her neck, and watched her pulse react. If a heart could smile, he knew his was beaming. "We have a house guest. It's gonna shock you, but Javier is at our house. He saved my ass, and his needed saving, so turnabout is fair play, right? Tomorrow, I'll tell you the whole story, but for now, rest, my beautiful wife." He kissed her hand again. "I love you and see you, mañana."

The last thing he wanted to do was leave her bedside, but he understood boundaries and respected the authority who told him not to stay too long. When he exited the room, Antoine was waiting in the hallway by the elevator. "The therapist told me you got her to respond. Maybe she'll come back to us eventually." Antoine smiled, but there wasn't any emotion behind it. "I heard you abandoned the project with WSM. I got the impression they expected you to extract the Prime Minister, but something went wrong." He shifted from leg to leg. "I assure you, I thought it was all on the up and up. Believe me—"

Babe interjected, "Cold day in Hell. I think you expected them to take me out; that's what I think. It was bullshit, the whole fucking thing. Did you wink-wink with King to eliminate me in an attack?"

Antoine's face transformed from a fake smile to stone cold. His blue eyes took on a steel-grey appearance. "Marine, if I wanted you dead, you'd be dead. Make no mistake in thinking I'll back down from you; not happening." The two men stared into each other's eyes, exchanging a non-verbal slug-fest. Babe understood, but Antoine knew the Marine could dispose of him just as easily; therefore, they were on a level playing field. The elevator doors opened, and Antoinette was getting ready to step out. "We are all leaving. Your girl has shown some signs of life, all thanks to this big guy," and he patted Babe's shoulder. *Don't fucking touch me, asshole.* He just smiled; there was no point in being disrespectful to her mother, although he had strong suspicions that she had orchestrated the ruse. *Fucking games, fucking civilians.*

Angelette was outside smoking a cigarette, leaning against the building with one foot perched against the bricks. She looked up at Babe, "So where do I go now?"

He kept walking and said over his shoulder, "Go back to wherever you came from." She stubbed the smoke and ran to join her aunt and uncle. *Good riddance* rang through his head. Once in the truck, he pounded the steering wheel. "And this is the bullshit that goes with relationships. What the fuck was I thinking? How'd I let myself fall in love?"

A few days went by, and he'd established a routine. Work out, check in with the boys, sign school papers or cut checks, shower, play with Chancée, visit Ruthie and Javier, and head to the hospital.

After returning from the hospital, Javier stopped him. "Marine, you remind me of my son's hamster on one of those wheels—going, going, going, and getting nowhere. Friend, you need an outlet besides working out. How is it with your wife? Progress?" He was back to the smooth, controlled man of distinction. The worry appeared to be a thing of the past. "Tonight, after your visit, we're going out."

Babe poured a cup of coffee and sat in one of the padded chairs in the family room. "She squeezes my hand and smiles sometimes. When I kiss her, I see changes in the monitors; it's just a matter of time." It was the first time he didn't feel tight like a violin string preventing a full breath. No, now he could fully expand his chest, quenching his blood's oxygen need. He knew she was getting better. Whether it took months or years, he would wait for her. In the meantime, he'd call Jarvis and maybe do a few rescues with him. Jarvis was the real deal, unlike the stooges from the Congo. They were dangerous because they lacked skill and knowledge and proudly displayed unimpressive machismo. There was no doubt he could have wiped out the entire group single-handedly. As far as he could tell, no one had any training. It was like a gang of neighborhood scoobies that would beat on their chest only to deflate when an authentic warrior challenged.

Javier got up and fixed a cocktail of the Marine's amber liquid. He took a swig. "Babe, you heard me. Tonight we go out. I know I've told you too much manly storage affects one's mind; I need some female company tonight." He glided across the room, sat in one of the padded chairs, and casually crossed his legs. "Any ideas? I'm not talking street hooker but well-trained, clean call-girl. I'm not in the mood to chat someone up in a bar. I want the real deal."

Babe laughed, "What? You've been here night after night with Ruthie and haven't made progress?" His chest rose and fell as he let go of a resounding bellow of laughter. He quietened because he didn't want to offend the old gal. "I can make a few calls. I know you have a crew in New Orleans; you told me as much. What about one of them?"

"No way, Marine. I want them scared shitless of me, and banging one of them isn't the way to maintain control." Ruthie walked into the room with the baby, who was screaming to beat the band.

She responded that the poor baby was suffering from colic and asked Babe to pump her legs. *Pump her legs?* The older woman realized he was confused and placed Chancée on the sofa. She told Babe to watch and learn. She softly spoke to the baby as she bent her knees and pushed her little legs toward her midsection. After a few presses, the baby released an audible toot. "Jesus, I'm supposed to make her fart? That's the trick?" He questioned in between chuckles.

"Sir, sweet little Chancée needed to drop a rose. What's wrong with you? Now, your boys they expel gas like grown men and are rude about it. I'd swat their bottoms, but who knows what would come out. Sir, they need you to straighten them out about uncouth behavior." She patted the baby's stomach and used her thumb and ring finger to squeeze her belly gently. "See, her stomach is soft, and all that painful gas is gone. You know now? This baby don't cry unless she's hungry, dirty, or bound with gas. Lesson over; take your child, sir; she misses you." She started to walk toward the laundry room but turned. "Oh, and sir, there's nothing wrong with my ears. Watch your words; you better put something substantial in the swear word jar and ask Gawd's forgiveness for, well, you know what." She continued to the laundry room.

Javier asked Babe again about the call girls. Juggling the baby, he dug the phone out of his pocket and pressed a few buttons. "Paula, this is Babe. Yes, ma'am, it has been a long time. I have a friend in town who might want to share a drink with you tonight. Is that a possibility?" He paused for a minute. "Yes, bring Scarlet with you and see y'all at ten Royal Hotel bar. Thank you, ma'am." He ended the conversation and looked at Javier, "You are such a bad influence on me. You're married, and so am I. It's wrong."

The two talked about what was happening with Colombian businesses, and it was like he'd said before: the Federales were moving in on operations, not to arrest but to cut out the competition. The carnage had been substantial with some of the other cartels. Plain and simple, he wanted out. Javier admitted he was fearful for his wife and children. They couldn't live an everyday life. Maria complained that Javier had them imprisoned in the house. He decided to hand over the business to Seb or one of his dedicated men. Once he'd completed the transaction, he'd join his family in Barcelona, where he could relax and live out the rest of his days. He had billions put away, all in cash. Life would be easy and grand.

Babe watched when Javier asked to hold Chancée. For being such a bad motherfucker, he was gentle, and maybe Trinity had been right; he was the one person that understood him and the demons. He heard the back door open, "Hey. Yo, Vic, you're home. Have I got the four-one-one for you." Chris was effervescent. "This boy here," and he puffed out his chest and poked his thumbs toward himself, adding to his already cocky personality, "Is going to LSU. It was in the mailbox. Here, look at the info. The other douchebags home yet?" Javier shifted his eyes toward Babe. Babe raised an eyebrow. "Sorry, I got my money for the jar. I've been waiting to hear back. Now we need to decide on dorm, meal plan, there's so much sh—stuff, but you can't drag your as—butt." Babe cleared his throat and glared at him. "Sorry. I'm excited. Fuck, yeah." Ruthie called from the kitchen, saying she heard it all; congratulations, but he owed the jar at least five dollars. He had two bucks and change. "I'll give you what I have and put an IOU for the rest." As he passed Javier, the visitor handed him a five, and he passed the baby back to her dad.

Babe waited until the other two came home, bantered about the day. They had gotten used to him being home, and their closeness bonded even more. When it came to Jacob, it was nothing short of hero worship. The youngster was hitting a growth spurt and was as tall as Reg but still had a little boy way about him. Babe wondered if the exploitation stunted him developmentally.

Twenty minutes later, the boys went to do their homework and left the men to talk. "Javier, I'm going by the hospital, so if you want to take Chris' car, I'll meet you at the Royal." Ruthie called from the kitchen and said she had dinner simmering on the stove and expected a full table. Javier looked down, his shoulders quivering as he tried to hold in the laughter. "We know who wears the pants in this family," he said with a subdued grin. "Yes, I'll take the boy's car. I might not be back until morning."

Reg fiddled with his phone at the dining table and, without looking up, commented, "Looks like someone's planning on getting lucky. Babe, maybe you should take a page out of his book." Still not looking up, both men looked at him.

Babe's eyebrows shot up. In a coarse whisper, he addressed Reg, "Listen, you little motherfucker, you owe my friend an apology, and get straight to your room. What the fuck is wrong with you?"

Reg shrugged his shoulder with his hands turned up. "I was just kidding." Looking at Javier, he apologized, "Sir, I meant no disrespect. I thought I was just pal-ing with the big dogs, but sorry, I guess I'm jealous; I've been going through a dry patch." Javier cracked up, and Babe's eyes popped open in surprise. Ruthie came from the kitchen with a dish towel over her shoulder, telling all three that she'd heard enough of their dirty mouths and that everybody owed the jar. She turned on her heel and walked into the kitchen with determined steps. Reg called into the kitchen, "Lovely Miss Ruthie, I meant no harm, and I'll gladly deposit some money when I have it." He rolled his eyes and, under his breath, said when pigs fly.

Dinner went smoothly; everyone left the table with a full stomach and compliments to the chef. Babe tried to tell Ruthie he was going to the hospital but might be late. She curled her lips in disapproval and said she heard and wondered what Miss Trinity thought about the rendezvous after the hospital. It hit a nerve.

Ruthie's comment weighed heavy on his heart, crushing it with shame. He'd stepped out on her already. How would he feel if he reversed the roles? His mind drifted to Carmen, then Angelette, even pretending it was Trinity, and then saying yes to another call girl; how cavalier? What Javi did was not the ticket to run with the boys. He had made vows. What kind of man was he? Javi was on his computer in the living room. "Amigo, I'm not going to the Royal. Cancel the other girl?" He asked.

"No. I got it." Babe's mind flashed back to the Spring Breakers and their sex parties and how it ended in the death of Jessica Lambert, one of the college students. Threesome stuff wasn't his jam.

WAKE FROM SLUMBER

Babe had worn a path from his house to the hospital. For the first time, there wasn't a parking spot for three blocks, so he grabbed the first one he could. Walking to see Trinity, his mind played back how he had changed. Emotions and feelings, once unfamiliar territory, were now commonplace. He was so deep in thought that he let down his guard, and the next thing he felt was a gun against his kidneys.

"Empty your pockets, gimme your watch and ring, now." The gunman ordered. Babe could sense the chump's size and that he was alone.

The big man growled his answer. "Hear me loud and clear, motherfucker, don't pick a fight you can't win."

"Pops, I got the gun. I'll—"

Before he could finish his sentence, Babe had disarmed him and punched him in the gut. The boy doubled over. "You're a kid. What the fuck is wrong with you? Do you not see I'm twice your size." The boy tried to catch his breath while choking and ultimately puking where he stood. "You need money, or is this some badass initiation? If so, tell your bros not to fuck with me. Got it, kid?" The boy had terror in his eyes. What he thought would be no big thing and easy ended up bigger than big, and his life was on the line.

With tears in his eyes, the assailant begged for his life. Babe cocked his head in puzzlement. He told the boy if he wanted him dead, he'd already be dead. Those words rang in his ears from the conversation with Antoine. It was a common thing to say for someone with a propensity for a violent life. Babe stretched his arm out, pointing down the street, and told him to go. Before walking into the hospital, he put the gun in his waistband. Even though distracted by the baby thug, Babe noticed that the Noelle's car was nowhere to be seen.

Security, nurses, aides, and even other families visiting their patients knew him by this time. One of the dads rode up in the elevator. Babe felt compelled to warn him of the dangers on the street. Where was this coming from? Suddenly, he was Mr. Chatty. *Shit*. Trinity's nurse ran up to him, and his heart dropped into his gut. In milliseconds, sweat poured from his body, and his face must have looked terrorized. The nurse quickly interjected, "No, no, nothing bad, sir. Trinity opened her eyes and fixed on objects around her. There was a connection. This is excellent progress." He let out a sigh. Gradually, his heart resumed to normal rhythm.

Babe lightly tapped on her door before opening it. The nurses had propped her up in the bed, and she watched as Babe walked in. There was recognition in her eyes, although she was non-verbal. He smiled with his typical half-cocked grin. "Look who's awake, my sleeping beauty." Her eyes had a glassy appearance, and she registered that she understood some of the things he had said. Her cognition was far from good, but she hadn't opened her eyes the day before, so she'd made progress. The NG tube was still in place, which seemed to aggravate her. "No, hot thing, don't pull." Her expression was blank. There were no signs of a smile or any emotion for that matter.

Babe pulled up a chair and leaned against the bedrail, resting his chin on his fist, petting her hand with his other. "There's a shitload to tell, so I'll begin with casual banter and polite catch-up. I told you about Javier being at our house. He's moving his family to Barcelona. That'll make a fun trip for our family. Speaking of, the boys are growing like weeds. Chris got an acceptance letter to LSU; the little fucker is excited about all the arrangements, like the dorm choice and all that shit. Ruthie has been helping out taking care of Chancée. God, Trinity, she's gonna be a beauty—a total mix of us. You know, since we met, you've opened my life to everything I missed as a boy. Part of me wants to say thanks for breaking open the cocoon around my emotions, but on the other hand, feelings are fucked up. Bam, they come from nowhere and knock you to your knees. You're probably sick of my jawing, but I don't know what to do with everything in my heart. One minute my heart feels like it's in a vice; the next, it feels like I'm gonna hurl or shit my pants; the cramping is undefinable. You know what, I'll just sit here, and we can look at each other. I'll be quiet." She closed her eyes and slowly moved her head to say no. "I guess that means you want me to talk. Jesus, I've never been a talker, and look at me now; I've caught the verbal diarrhea from you." A corner of her mouth twitched like a smile. "I see; we're telling jokes now. My girl, you are getting better by the second. The nurses told me not to stay too long, that it would tire you, and that's before you woke up. I'm gonna sit here and let you sleep.

"I have a Bible app on my phone. King David and I have a lot of similarities; I know I already told you that. From what I gather, he wasn't a big dude, and well, enough said about that, but he was badass, yet he won favor with God. Okay, so I've accepted there's a God. How can you not when you look at our beautiful baby girl? She's perfect. Wait, I have a picture of her from this morning." He scrolled his phone and held it so she could see. A single tear meandered down the side of her face onto the pillow. "Maybe I shouldn't have shown you; I'm sorry. Trinity, I don't know what the fuck I'm supposed to do or say." With a slight movement, she moved her thumb along the hand holding hers.

Her touch sent shivers through his body like when he watched her at Louie's before getting the nerve up to speak to her. An adjustment in his pants required immediate attention. "You got my fighting man at attention, and it was a tiny touch on my hand. I remember the first time you came to my place in that flimsy dress. I could see your nipples. The dress barely stayed on your body, and your head was full of thick, wild black hair. You wanted me as much as I wanted you."

The sound of someone clearing their throat penetrated the moment. "Sir, she needs rest." She glanced at the monitors and her pulse rate had skyrocketed. "She's waking up for sure, but not in a rush—slowly. Time to leave; we will see you tomorrow." He wanted to say the reason her pulse was up had nothing to do with healing but that she had been a sexual creature before, and he'd aroused her. Some things were best left unsaid. He kissed her forehead, whispering how much he wanted her and how she needed to get better for a rocking adventure between the sheets. Her pulse went up again. "Sir," the nurse repeated. Had she any idea what he'd whispered to his wife, they'd probably ban him from the hospital.

Driving down St. Charles, he could only think about making love to her. He knew she wasn't well enough to bear his weight, but maybe he could give her pleasure with his touch. He turned on the radio to distract him. *When A Man Loves A Woman, are you fucking kidding me?* He didn't want to go home to an empty bed, so he passed by Louie's.

Samantha screeched across the bar, "Oh, my Gawd! Finn," she called out to the far side of Louie's. Babe smiled to himself, watching Finn ignore her. It was apparent he'd had his fill of Samantha for the evening, and it wasn't even nine-thirty. A girl Babe hadn't seen before let Finn know Sam had called him. His response was nothing short of whatever.

Once finished bussing the tables, he made his way back to the bar. "Samantha, I'm not the busser; get the new kid out of the bathroom to do his job."

"Look who's here." Finn turned his head, then did a double take. He moved quickly around the bar and did the one-armed man hug with the big guy.

"It is great to see you, Big Man. I never did get to tell you how sorry I wasn't more on top of the Trin—" Finn seemed older, more mature, not the boy busser with a massive crush on his woman. Finn seemed more of a man than a boy. Perhaps the horrible encounter with the crazy siblings of Marky, the deranged Amazonian welder, had changed his point of view.

"I get it, Finn," Babe told him. "Truth be told, I shouldn't have trusted her to stay home and not come to work. No one here is at fault except the psycho bitch and her brother, but they're history." He chucked him on the shoulder. "Now, can I get a drink? I don't want to deal with Samantha tonight or any night for that matter."

Babe sat at the first open seat at the bar. Sam abandoned anyone other than Babe. She stood with her hand on her hip, batted her eyes and puckered her lips. "Ma-rine, you lookin' good, boy. It's a shame about poor Trinity, but I took over." She winked at him. Finn placed the two-finger pour of Glenlivet in front of Babe and mentioned the guys at the end of the bar were looking for her. She rolled her eyes and left.

Towel tucked in his pants and crossing his arms in front of him, Finn said, "Babe, things here are same old, same old. Still, knocking it out of the park in school and almost done. I've decided to go into law and am taking some pre-law classes. Hey, are you still a lawyer? I need to get some rec letters." Babe affirmed and offered to write a glowing reference. He told Finn he needed to start thinking about what kind of law he wanted. The conversation was interrupted by drink orders. Finn made his way back to the big guy. "I know they make bank, but I'm not interested in ambulance chasing if that's what you're wondering. I don't need this mug on billboards," pointing to his face with a cheesy smile. "Maybe clerk at the DA's office. I think I want prosecutorial rather than defense. Get the bad guys. You know a bit about that, huh, Hulk?" Babe sipped his drink, raised an eyebrow, and nodded, saying yes. "I gotta say, not trying to sound gay, but I miss the times before you married Trinity. The whole feeling of the place has changed."

Babe swallowed the last of his tumbler and said he understood. "Life takes us on some weird ass journeys. You need to stay the course, get out of school, and get out of here. Not that it hasn't been great to see you, but you're too intelligent to stay here and don't tell me its cause of anything to do with—" he tilted his head toward Samantha.

Finn smirked, "Fu-heck no. Sam has made Louie's her own trick stop. She's blown more guys than a circus clown making balloon animals. I'm seeing the girl I brought to your wedding, and before you say it, yes, she looks like Jessica from Spring Break. Sometimes when I think about those breakers, I get angry about all the crazy shit that night" He turned to mix a couple of cocktails for two men sitting next to Babe. "Hey, Trey and Max come in occasionally asking about you and Trinity. Have you heard about the Jack the Ripper guy prowlin' the night? They call him the City Slasher. He's gotten three women so far, all prostitutes. Trey and Max are on it like flies on shit."

Hm. Interesting, he thought. Babe remarked that he hadn't heard about the murders. Maybe he found a new pastime for the late hours of the night.

The screen on his phone lit up with a text. It was the nurse taking care of Trinity.

Nurse: She said your name. Come back.

Babe: Roger that.

Maybe it was a fluke, and maybe it wasn't. He was taking no chances of missing out on a word or two. "Finn, this has been fun, but the hospital calls. Tell Trey and Max I send my regards, oh, and give Shep my best." He stood, put a ten on the bar, and exited.

Trying to get out of the Quarter was obnoxious. Traffic was bumper to bumper, and a few streets had barricades. "What the fuck is going on?" he said aloud to himself. As traffic stopped next to a barricade, he looked over and saw Max. He put the window down and could feel tingles in his stomach. His breathing picked up, and his senses went on high alert. "Max," he shouted.

"Where y'at, Babe." Max leaned on the door. Finn was right; not much changed. The detective looked the same as he did the first time he met him. "We got a manhunt going on. A pedestrian crossed an alley and saw a man in the act of raping one of the girls of the night. They screamed, startling the guy, and he bolted, but we think we got him boxed in. Trey is playing the role of a bloodhound and following the tracks. Unfortunately, the working girl didn't make it. His numbers are stacking up and fast. Wanna help special ops man? We just made it mandatory that doors be locked. No in and no out. The businesses aren't too happy, but whatcha gonna do?"

Babe stared straight ahead as the traffic started to roll. "I would, but can't. The nurse called and told me to come right away; Trinity said her first word since—" A lump developed in his throat as though tears were on the way. Max said he got him covered and moved the barricade so he could skirt the traffic. He said nobody would stop him on his way out of the area; he'd radio ahead. "If y'all are still looking for the fucker when I leave the hospital, I'll help. Thanks, Max. Put some officers on balconies and roofs; it's a better angle." Max saved him a good half hour, letting him pass. He hauled ass to Trinity.

Maybe it was the late hour when most people were chillin' or hanging at the Royal for two call girls. *Javier.* For some reason, his affair with Carmen didn't conjure any emotion. He thought Trinity was dead or on death's doorstep, he'd been through a ton of shit, and it meant nothing. It was a good release of pent-up energy. She was a lovely lady and beautiful beyond words, but it was no big thing. Now that Trinity was waking up, he'd let those dogs lie unless she specifically asked; there was no point in hurting her for something one step above pulling his pud. There was a parking place big enough for his truck square in front of the entrance.

Mitchell, the doorman, waved him inside. "Back again? Go on up;

you're the only visitor right now. I haven't seen anyone else but you all day. Enjoy your time, and I hope your wife is on the mend. When University Medical transferred her, I was on duty." He crossed himself. "I didn't hold up much hope, I'm afraid to say." Babe stepped into the elevator as the doors opened, and Mitchell returned to his seat at the table by the front door.

The unit was dim, and only two nurses were at the station. Emotions started welling up as the nurse came to him with a smile. Major acrobatics twisted in his stomach as they approached each other. "Mr. Vicarelli, she said Babe, clear as a bell, no exaggeration, swear." She raised her right hand as though giving testimony in a trial. *Pretty funny.* A thought ricocheted through his brain. He wondered if her parents had visited, but the doorman said he'd been the only visitor. *Note to self: check the visitor log on the way out.*

When he reached her door, he turned and thanked the nurse for calling him. He lightly rapped, and then he heard the most glorious thing. She spoke, "Yes?" There was no holding the tears back. His girl was returning from the dead. As he stepped in, he saw a look of recognition in her eyes, and the twinkle, while not as sparkling, was present. "Babe." Tears tumbled from both their eyes.

"Oh, ma girl. I have missed you." He pulled up a chair and leaned on the bedside rail. "Can I kiss you? I won't bother the tube." She nodded, and he gently kissed the side of her lips.

They stared at each other, looking deep into their souls. She touched the tube. "Out." Her voice was like a gravelly whisper. She'd been asleep for a long time. Trinity held his hand, then placed her tiny balled-up fist inside his palm, his fingers reflexively wrapped around hers. Babe pressed the call button. Response time was remarkable, of course; as far as he knew, she was one of two on the floor. Trinity pointed to the tube. "Out." She followed the tube with her fingers around her ear.

"I'll see what I can do, but it'll probably be tomorrow morning. Do you want something to help you sleep? I know you've been sleeping, but the state of consciousness was different. Now, you need as much rest as possible. Big strides tonight, something to cheer about." She said she'd be back in a bit.

Trinity continued to have puzzlement in her eyes. What was she confused about? Was it the attack or her condition, and what should he tell her? Safe bet, the baby. He could talk a long mile about Chancée. He told her about the nursery and its appearance, then showed her pictures. Babe had dozens of photos of the baby in his Camera Roll. Warmth came from his deepest part as he handed his phone to her for a gander of the pictures. She looked with love, kissed her fingertips, and touched the phone, which displayed an up-close shot of the baby. Her face filled the screen, and her eyes were focused as though sending a message. Trinity closed her eyes and held the phone to her heart. Silent tears trickled down her cheeks. When she opened her eyes, she pointed a finger and whispered, "You."

Babe nodded. "She's a combo. Our princess parlayed the best of us into one beautiful package. She's feisty but always smiling, well, mostly. She has happy eyes, like yours, only my color. I don't know what you remember from my non-stop verbosity while you slept. It will take time, ma girl, and I know patience is not one of your gifts, but you must be; do I make myself clear?" She slowly smiled, eyes darting through space, then focused on him and replied crystal. "And that, dear, is the perfect answer. Roger that." After another forty-five minutes, the nurse called it over for the night. It had been a much-needed visit for both of them, and he couldn't stop feeling she'd turned a corner, which might intensify her recovery. Before he left, he asked the nurse about bringing the baby in the morning. To his surprise, she said yes.

Driving down St. Charles Avenue, one would have thought her responsiveness would put him on cloud nine. Such was not the case; in fact, if anything, it made him lonelier and more impatient. Looking at the time, he figured Javier was getting his money's worth and then some. Two women, at the same time, were not the least bit sexy to him. He wasn't ever the type to look for sex with more than he and one other, not group or orgy style—raw and primal. His little woman and he were the perfect couple for lovemaking; she was equally into sex with a purpose. The gentleness of sweet caresses or pillow talk came before or after.

"What the hell? He'll either ignore the call and think I've lost my mind or answer because he completed the mission." One ring. Two rings. Three rings. *Ignore the call.*

On the fourth ring, he picked up. "Marine, you change your mind? If so, too late. I gave your piece to some twenty-something kid at the bar. He was down for the opportunity and thanked me. Both are pretty girls; good taste, my friend. I'm going to sleep at the hotel, and I'll see you in the morning, probably after your workout." After a brief hesitation, as though he'd debated asking the question, he spoke, "How was your lady? Any improvement?"

Babe responded that she had made great strides, but it made him miss her even more. Javier commented about a shower and whether he was right-handed or left-handed. Babe quickly shut the conversation down and said he'd see him in the morning. Somehow, those needs didn't even register on the give-a-shit-o-meter; his concentration was interacting with her in a real conversation, not just a word here or there, but at least it was an improvement. The death mask was gone. *It's just a matter of time.*

BACK TO BUSINESS

*P*olice presence covered every viable option for escape within a six-block radius. If they didn't flush him out, they'd increase the perimeter. Trey's phone buzzed. "Nothing yet, Max; you'll know when we get him." The new captain, James "Big Jim" Campbell, was determined to make his mark and went balls out on the manhunt positioned for maximum coverage. He was determined to catch the bastard while earning cred among the rank and file.

Even though the hotel garage was well-lit as sensibly possible, there was no such thing as a murder-free zone. The lighting merely gave a false sense of security. The attendant, Jude, a young man, heard a shrill scream. He radioed his boss, reporting the situation. The two other attendants jumped in a motorized guest service cart, flying through the garage. A man and a woman came into view, pointing to a dark corner near the elevators—a horrific scene presented. A young woman, maybe early twenties, sliced ear to ear, was posed, pointing to the elevator. In each of the murders, the killer had posed the victims, pointing to a way out that the girls missed.

The head of security was on Jude's heels and skirted around quickly, getting to the scene. There was no point in feeling for a pulse; she was dead, so he made the dreaded call.

THE IMPOSTOR LIE

"Nine-one-one, what's your emergency?" said the voice on the other end of the call.

"We have a dead woman—"

The emergency operator informed the head of hotel security the police were aware and on the scene.

In exasperation, he audibly sighed into the phone. "No, ma'am, no police here; it must be a different victim." Slashing a throat was deadly and fast, giving the murderer an easy minute to escape. Did the hand pointing to the bank of elevators mean the slasher was in the hotel? "The victim is on the third level in the Royal parking garage by the elevators; send someone right away."

The dispatch sent the info, and the words "another victim" rang throughout the radio. Max contacted Captain Campbell and said he was close to the Royal and would take the call. Then he called Trey to let him know they had another victim; he wasn't sure if it involved the manhunt, but it was too much of a coincidence, and neither detective believed in the myth of coincidence. The alley slaying was sloppy, nothing methodical like the others, but being spied on by witnesses, he finished the deed and vanished. Knowing the location of the first murder set an uncomplicated path to the Royal through entrances and exits, avoiding the streets. Even though it was a bit like closing the barn door after the horses escaped, the captain sent orders for all places of businesses to lock all entrances and exits. Maybe they had him trapped somewhere, but that presented dozens of possibilities.

Max pulled up, blocking the parking lot exit ramp. Jude was back at his stand. "Hey kid, any cars leave in the past half hour?" His gruffness was off-putting, and Jude responded no with trepidation in his voice. "You seen anyone on foot around here?" He answered, no, sir. The angst in the department was palpable, especially with Big Jim breathing down their necks.

Max called Trey, who answered, "I told you—"

"No, it's not that. We got another one in the garage at the Royal. The doer must have been rushed with the hooker in the alley and didn't have time to play with the corpse, sick piece of shit. I guess he didn't fill his appetite. Two in one night; he's on a spree, dat's real, son. Same M.O., slashed ear to ear and staged. If, and that's a big if, he's indicating how he left, he's in the hotel. Fat fucking chance of finding him."

The parking attendant, Jude, was freaked out. His whole body trembled. While they spoke, a teenage boy, maybe fifteen, walked down the ramp like he was looking for someone. Max stopped him and asked where he was coming from or going. The boy claimed he was looking for his parents. Something about the kid triggered a memory, one Max couldn't identify. He flipped through a pictorial in his mind. Discreetly, he snapped a photo of the boy. Maybe Trey would recognize him. With nothing to hold him on, security let him into the hotel to find his parents. The teen was five-eight, slender build, shaggy hair wisping from under a Saints ball cap, nothing to write home about, but Max had an uneasy feeling. Could he be the slasher? Most of the hookers could've taken him; they were a rough bunch of girls.

The signal wasn't good in the garage, and the photo took forever to get through to Trey.

Trey: What about him?

Max: Just saw him, and he looks familiar.

Trey: Couple years ago. Kid was being abused by mom's boyfriend, who ended up getting his throat cut in kitchen. Mom worked a pole. That's the kid.

Max: We got the ID of first victim? I wonder if the kid killed the boyfriend, snapped, and now we have the slasher. Maybe vic #1 was mom. Just a thought.

Trey: Find the kid and hold him.

Max didn't come across as an intellectual, but his instincts and gut check were usually spot on. Trey saw the Captain a block over. It was worth checking into Max' theory.

THE IMPOSTOR LIE

Babe pulled into Hotel Noelle and parked. He made it to the corner where Max had been in double time. There was a uniformed officer in his place. "Where's Max?"

"Sir, all guests are to stay in their hotels. Where are you staying?" He looked up at the big man.

"No disrespect. I know what's going on, and I'm here to help. Where's Max?" He texted Trey quickly.

Babe's phone buzzed. "Max is at the Royal. The guy hit two in one night. Sledge has a gut saying it was a kid from an incident two or so years ago. Freakin' pedo trying to hose his girlfriend's kid. We never got the impression he was the doer at the time. Lemme talk to Reynolds." Babe handed his phone to the uniformed officer, who responded to Trey by saying he understood.

Not that the policeman had been abrasive or anything negative, but he was much friendlier after speaking with Trey. He was a working stiff doing his job, and the Marine had nothing against that or the officer. "Detective Sledge is at The Royal. Know where it is?" Babe smiled and said yes. "Sorry—"

"Officer, nothing to be sorry about. Stay safe." Babe turned and headed toward The Royal to meet up with Max. He had to straighten the situation about the pedophile murder; he knew it wasn't the kid. Of course, he did; it was his own handiwork, but it might have traumatized the boy, and now he blamed anyone who might have resembled his mother. Maybe that hadn't been the first time the boyfriend assaulted the kid. One thing was for sure: it was his last attempt, and Babe cut him ear to ear.

The French Quarter felt odd and desolate, almost like during a hurricane; the only faces were law enforcement, which lent an eery cast to the night. His spidey senses were on high alert with blown-out pupils, more intense respirations, and dryness in his mouth. It was his hope that it wasn't the boy; the kid had nothing to do with the slasher, but if it were him, that piece might fit flawlessly. It was scary what abuse could do to a young mind. Hell, he was a prime example. Until Trinity, the psych community viewed him as sociopathic even though they hadn't recorded it in his medical records. No one had to spell it out for him. Babe knew he was a serial killer; whether he could convince himself they had been righteous kills was more the matter at hand. Of the countless lives he'd taken, whether in combat or urban streets, there were only three he felt wrong and guilty. They'd probably haunt him to the grave.

Max looked to his left as a giant ominous figure turned into the parking garage and approached. It caused him to put his hand on his weapon and suck in a deep breath. When the light from one of the lamps illuminated the person, he breathed a sigh of relief. "You, motherfucker, almost got shot where you stood. Good to see you, Marine."

"Right back atcha. By the way, I know for a fact the boy didn't kill his mother's pedophile boyfriend because I know who did, but the dude's long gone, maybe even dead. That's not to say that if the boy saw the gruesome scene, it couldn't have warped him into a psychosis. Abuse can do strange things to people. No one ever comes out whole." He put his hand on Max' shoulder, who was just shy of a foot shorter than him.

After all the research Babe had done, it was conclusive the victims of abuse led to abusers. There was no doubt in his mind his abusive father had much to do with the person he turned out to be. It took someone like Trinity to fit into the keyhole of his heart and release emotions pent up for years. Sometimes, the emotion was more than he could handle. He needed the key to his heart back in his life. He asked Max if he wanted him to search the parking lot. The detective said the boy, according to parking attendants, entered the hotel, and the rest of the hotel was on lockdown.

The two took the stairs leading to registration; one turned right and the other left, but before parting ways, Babe asked Max to copy him on the picture. No doubt it was the same boy from two years before. He walked to the right, passing a lounge packed with guests. He strolled through the crowd; it would have been an easy place to blend. Because of the lockdown, guests of all ages packed in like sardines. Javier was in the corner at a table by himself. Babe sat in an open chair at the table.

"Well, look what the cat drug in. Glenlivet? How about something a bit more classy?" Javier was the picture of sophistication, relaxed in the chair, one leg crossed over the other and an elbow on the arm of the chair, cupping a snifter of brandy between his fingers. He took a long, deep breath, savoring the aromatic pleasure of the fine libation. "Marine, this is divine. What brings you here? Don't tell me you're the—"

"No, sir. I like working ladies. Each has a story to tell. You seen this boy?" He flashed the photo to his friend.

"You're fucking with me now. How'd you know?" Babe leaned in closer and asked knew what. "That's the young man I offered the high-priced call girl. The entertainment stoked the boy. She was one cute girl. You missed out, my friend. She would have sucked your dick so hard your eyeballs would have sunken. Muy bonita. Luscious full lips, long blonde hair to tickle your balls. But, that young man had an evening delight. Snooze, you lose." All he was missing was a fat Cuban cigar. Babe noticed every woman took a long gander at his Colombian friend. A few checked him out, but Javier was svelte and cosmopolitan.

"Lucky for him, unlucky for her. I'm betting the young man is the slasher, and you gave him a victim on a silver platter." Javier's face dropped. He truly was saddened. "Maybe not; I didn't see the victim. First, I want to find him, then I'll check on girl two for the night." Javier gave up his seat, and the two men scanned the lounge. No luck.

They headed out to the Mezzanine. They saw him leaning against the side of one of the grand arched windows. Javier approached him first. He wouldn't have rattled the boy; after all, he was the man who bought him a roll with a call girl. The boy turned toward Javier as Babe came from behind. The boy might have told the police Babe was the killer of his mother's boyfriend. Remembering the night, the Marine thought the boy looked like he was in shock and probably not able to identify him, but it was risky. Javier asked, "How was your special time with your beautiful lady friend?"

The boy was startled when Babe cleared his throat. "Mister, you almost gave me a heart attack." He grabbed his chest. Babe noticed a small bloodstain on the boy's wrist. He answered Javier, "Uh, she was great. Thanks. My mother will start blowing up my phone if I don't get home, but the Quarter is on lockdown."

Babe leaned into his ear and told him maybe he should call and let her know. The boy jumped a mile again and, upon seeing the size of the man behind him, became shaky. The younger stared at him in the eyes and said he'd seen him before at Louie's, and Finn had told him everyone called him The Hulk. The boy was the new busser. *Is that where you know me from?* Babe mused. *Are we playing a game?* Maybe that was so, but there was too much coincidence with him coming in from the parking garage. Babe needed to take a look at the victim.

"What were you doing in the parking garage?" Babe queried.

"Screwing the girl your friend turned me on to." Babe pressed where. "Look, I don't have a room or an apartment I can take someone to, so we grabbed the back of a pickup truck. Once we finished, I jumped out and headed into the hotel, hoping to leave through the front door and be on my way home." The next question was why he wasn't at Louie's. The kid said Shep cut him when all the freaky rumors started buzzing, and guests hurried to leave. Babe had to admit, it made sense. But what was the blood on the wrist about? The boy licked his finger and wiped, saying it was probably ketchup; he had no idea. Either the kid was fucking stone cold, or he wasn't the doer. Just then, Max walked up, huffing and puffing.

"Ah, you got the fucker." He began to Mirandize him and hitched the cuffs on him. "Figured you'd find him. I tell ya, Babe, you are in the wrong business. You'd make a bitchin investigator." Javier chuckled. He looked at the smooth Latino who could have easily stepped out of a fashion magazine. "You a friend of Babe's?"

Javier put out his hand, "I am. Name's Chaz Estrando." Javier's eyes were cold and black; if one looked into them, it might send shivers up their spine. Babe noted his friend was one mean motherfucker, a no-nonsense kind of beast. They made the ideal frenemies, both intimidating and all out of give-a fucks.

"I want to see the crime scene; can you radio I'm coming?" Babe asked Max.

"Yeah, but why; it ain't gonna tell you nothin', but go for it, big guy, just don't contaminate the scene, move anything, or get in the way of the Crime Lab." He turned to face his cuffed suspect. "We're going to the station for a little chat." He radioed Trey, "Kimble, got a suspect. The kid from two years ago." Max escorted the young man to one of the uniformed officers with instructions to stay with him until he returned.

Babe followed and asked the kid, "What color and make was the truck?"

The boy looked shaken to the core. Not a guilty look to Babe, but maybe it was just an act. He answered a dark Ford.

Walking up the ramp, Babe scanned the parked vehicles. There was nothing to match the description on the first ramp. He couldn't imagine the boy taking his gift much further, but there wasn't a truck on the second level. Turning on the next ramp, he saw the yellow tape, elevator sign, and swarm of busy techs. The body was still present. Bingo! A big Ford truck was parked next to the elevator. *How convenient.* Maybe he had read the situation wrong, and it was possible, if not probable, that the kid was the slasher or, at the very least, had seen or heard something after getting his jollies. His senses had to be on high alert while doing the nasty in a well-traveled parking garage. It wasn't every day a boy like him got a free tumble with a high-price lady of the night.

Unfortunately, the victim was Paula. Babe knew her well, and she was a sweet kid who was working her way through college. She could work two nights and have enough money for all her bills and cash for food and partying with her friends. Her ensemble didn't scream professional—no glitter, sequins, or fishnets. What'd the boy do? Get his game on, then slice her throat? From the amount of blood at the scene, it was evident it was the point of attack. It still didn't compute. Thinking back at some of his targets, he could have sat and had dinner after the execution with no problem or been hauled to the police station and remained together. He knew why he did what he did. His casualties were more predators than victims.

Simply put, he was a more ruthless and cunning predator. They met their match and then some. The kid was bound to know something, given the proximity. Another weird emotion popped up—disappointment. He was disappointed in the kid. After saving his ass, literally, he took the new opportunity and turned into a raping, murderous sack of shit. Hopefully, Babe hadn't been the catalyst for the behavior.

A shade of melancholy washed over him. Javier was back at the corner table and had a cocktail in front of an empty chair. "You entertaining?" he asked before sitting.

"No, waiting for you, and I think you'll like the bourbon." Babe touched it to his lips and slowly sipped, sucking the unusual spirit between his teeth. He smiled and nodded. "So, was the kid guilty, and was it Paula, the blonde?"

Babe looked into his glass with a set jaw. "Yes, it was Paula. All indicators point to the boy. She did him in the bed of a truck right next to the elevators, proximity to the body." He clammed up. Javier pressed, saying there was more to the story. After another bourbon in his belly, he told the story of the boy, the pole dancing mother and pedo boyfriend. Javier nodded as he listened. Babe sat silent for a few moments. "I never have an audience, if you get my drift, and it's always been a predator getting eaten by this bigger predator," he pointed to himself. Babe slouched comfortably in the chair. The rigidity once pinning him to the chair had vacated his body. The Bourbon was excellent and brought on a relaxing effect. The release of his usually tight body stirred reflections of intimate times with Trinity. At times, it felt like he could melt under her touch. She was his kryptonite. It was the only time he felt his muscles melt.

Javier watched as Babe drifted somewhere. He knew about the Marine's demons and PTSD. He knew Babe had seen and done things that would make the average Joe's skin crawl or invoke instantaneous vomiting, but his planned tortures and executions topped Babe's. The media had exposed the inhumane actions of the cartel, so Javier's were far more hideous and premeditated, like skinning, burning, and boiling traitors or competitors alive. The occupants of the house of men boasted about how tenacious and vicious their boss was. Yet, Javier cast an appearance of cool, calm, and totally together. The gentle, sophisticated demeanor, while not an act, spoke to the insidiousness of his soul, not that Babe was in any position to judge. Questioning himself, *what was my most hideous elimination?*

"Marine, I don't know where the hell you go, but it's strange as all shit. You shut down. I'm not sure you breathe. You should see someone about your PTSD." Javier looked over the rim of his glass as he took a sip, waiting for an eruption, but he was one of the only people who could throw that alphabet diagnosis in Babe's face and not get put down like a rabid dog. It amazed Babe that Javier didn't feel guilt about anything. He had expressed fear for his family's safety but regrets he had none. He was one cold-hearted bastard; as the old saying goes, it takes one to know one.

He cocked his head and leaned into Javier, "Do you think I won't deal with my demons? News flash: I've tried. My nightmares aren't only from the military, but childhood, cartel shit, and all I want to do is make a difference. When you said that the police were correct, a serial killer was stalking the city, but they didn't know I was under their nose; they called me in for interrogation, guised as assisting them, but the Marines taught me how to work an interrogation to my favor. Unlike you, my Colombian kingpin, I'm suffocated in a cocoon of guilt, not necessarily from the things I've done but for the shitheads that got away or crimes I didn't stop. Until Trinity, I didn't process emotion or speak much." His tone turned sarcastic, "Excuse me if I zone. I'm a thoughtful man, always have been."

A polished gentleman entered. He had a look of importance and appeared to search the crowd. He turned his head toward Babe, and his eyes lit up. The property Manager was looking for a man the police described in perfect detail. Babe knew he stood out from the crowd, even sitting at a table in the corner sipping expensive bourbon with a friend.

As he approached the table, Babe became curious. What message was he delivering? The answer came fast. "Are you Captain Vicarelli?" He wasn't serving any longer; couldn't they drop the inappropriate formality? Babe nodded as he sipped the bourbon. "Detective Kimble asked me to look for you. He's waiting in the parking lot."

Babe stood and tilted his head as if to say, see what I mean, then patted Javier on the shoulder before following the manager. The Manager stayed alongside Babe until parting at the entrance to the garage. He exited and followed the ramp to the scene.

Trey met him, "I meant to ask you earlier how Trinity was doing. I've passed by Louie's to get updates, but never much info. And the baby?" Babe pulled out his phone and proudly displayed shots. "Dang, she looks like you, but I can see Trinity too." The police expanded the crime scene, and yellow tape included the truck. "This murder spree is something else. Max has doubts about the boy but brought him in any way. The crime lab found a used condom in the bed of the truck. They're taking it for testing. Looking at the victim, I've seen her before, but she's no street hooker. The boy spent a pretty penny for an hour with her."

Babe disclosed the boy didn't pay; it was a gift. Trey asked how he knew that hot tip. The big guy shrugged and said he just knew things and smiled.

WRONG PLACE, WRONG TIME

*M*ax checked his rearview mirror, observing his passenger in the back of his car. The boy looked terrified, which brought some doubt to the detective's mind. Was the kid in the wrong place at the wrong time a coincidence? Not that he leaned toward the notion of coincidence; the truth of the matter was, it smacked of it.

"Hey, kid, what you so nervous about? Did you kill? Never mind, we'll talk at the station. If you ain't guilty, you shouldn't be so damn nervous, just sayin'." Max tipped his head from side to side like it was on a spring, wrinkling his forehead while raising his eyebrows.

The boy dropped his head to his chest, completely done and in total surrender. All he was guilty of was trying to pick a few pockets of the rich people at The Royal, then lucked out on a paid-for high-priced hooker. The girl was pretty and didn't look like the hookers he saw on the corner of Decatur and Canal. She was funny, and he wished they could have been friends. At sixteen, his best guess was she might be eighteen. Under different circumstances, there could be alternatives to their friendship; she seemed to like his performance, but that could have been just an act. He would've wanted to kiss her but knew that wasn't on the menu.

The radio continued with a broken conversation. The word murder bounced around as though they were talking about buying a burger at

McDonald's. The boy in the backseat hoped the victim they talked about on the radio wasn't the blonde call girl. The word on the street was hookers were dropping like flies; there was a new serial murderer only targeting ladies of the night.

They pulled up to the precinct, where he had to relinquish his wallet and phone. Max handed back the phone, "You got one call." He had no one to call except Shep at Louie's.

The feisty owner picked up. "Shep, it's Boyd. I got brought into the police station, and I got no one to call but you." He swayed from foot to foot with tenuous nervous energy. His voice began to crack as he answered his boss' questions. "I got no idea why." He hemmed and hawed. Reluctantly he confessed, "I was working the rich people at The Royal when some guy offered me a hooker for free. I didn't have nowhere to take her, so I made use of a truck bed. That's it; I didn't do nothin' else, swear."

Boyd could hear the exasperation in Shep's voice. "Okay, here's what you do. I can't get to you, but there's this man; his name is Babe Vicarelli. He's tight with the cops and has a way of getting things done. The big guy is my niece's husband. Ask them to call him, and good luck Boyd."

Once the call was over, Max walked Boyd to Interrogation, uncuffed him, and shut the door. As he was closing it, the boy asked Max if he knew Babe and said Shep told him to ask them to call the guy. Max rubbed his temples and said sure to the kid.

Half an hour later, a massive man came through the door, the same one that had scared the crap out of him at the hotel. By this time, it was nearing three-thirty in the morning. "Okay, so I'm here. Who told you to call me, and what do you want?" The muscle man was menacing, and the kid began contemplating the wisdom of asking for him. Babe pulled up a chair sitting next to Boyd. He listened to the kid's fears, questions, and concerns. No one had told the boy why they arrested him. "First thing, you're not arrested. They brought you in for questioning. I'm sure you're aware of the serial killer at large. You, kiddo, chose the wrong place to bang the girl, and evidently, the killer was hiding out in the parking garage, got off on watching you with the girl, and then killed her after you left. I don't know if he approached her, and she thought she'd make a few more dollars or what. Did you hear anything weird when you left the parking garage? A scuffle or a scream?"

The boy dropped his head, looking forlorn. "Only tire screeches. Maybe a woman screamed, but it sounded like tires; I don't know. I was still floating after, well, you know, sex. I don't get laid very much, and a hooker was a first for me. I hope not my last." Obviously, Boyd didn't remember Babe as the man who stopped his mother's boyfriend from raping him and then watched as the man sliced his throat. In some ways, the boy reminded him of one of his kids at home. If Chris were sitting in the hotseat, what questions would he ask or advice impart? The suspect had the balls to fuck a working girl for sure, but not to kill her. He was easy pickings for the police to think they had the slasher. Case done. Caput. Closed, the new captain instantly became a hero.

There was a knock on the door, and then it opened; it was Trey. He looked shocked when he saw Babe. "What you doing here, big guy?"

"I'm Boyd's attorney. What are the charges?" Babe had an expressionless face. Trey quickly realized he was serious.

The detective sat, opened his notepad, and clicked his clickety pen. "According to your I.D., your name is Boyd G. Day, and you are sixteen, which means I'm gonna ship your ass to Florida Parishes Juvie unless the judge says, they're gonna try you as an adult because of the vicious and numerous murders."

Babe leaned forward on the table, and the boy started to sputter, "Close your mouth," he ordered the boy. "Detective, why did y'all bring him in? What evidence do you have on my client?"

Trey stared Babe eye to eye, "Fuck, Babe. You know damn well what for. This is not the first time your client," and he used air quotes, "has been close to a slashed throat. A couple of years ago, Boyd was in his mother's residence when her boyfriend got sliced across the neck. I think there may have been sexual abuse, according to Boyd's explanation, and out of nowhere, some guy came in and stopped the would-be abuse and killed the boyfriend." Trey bounced a nod, "Strange as it sounded, we bought the story at the time, but I'm not so sure now."

The boy was vibrating like a powder keg ready to blow. Babe told him to calm down and shut the fuck up. Babe drew the side of his mouth upward, squinting his eye at the same time. "I remember the incident. This boy did not kill the molester; I know."

Trey's eyebrows shot up, "Oh, you do? How?"

"I'd seen a guy hanging outside the mom's apartment. My place was around the corner. He's long gone, probably dead. Blood spray fanned on his face and clothes. I minded my business and kept to myself, like usual. The boy stumbled down the street, hailing a cab. The man was a real scuzzbucket."

Tensions ran high; the city couldn't withstand more bad press. As it was, New Orleans was in the top five cities for murder per capita. The media had donned the killer as The City Slasher, splashing the story all over local and national news. Any killing was horrible, but this predator was on a spree, not wasting any time between victims, almost taunting the police. The city was rife with sex workers, so a couple missing here or there didn't dent the call girls and guys, and there was always a plethora of murders from drug deals gone bad, love triangles, or gang violence.

Two minutes later, one of the beat cops radioed they were following a suspect. The clothing matched the passers-by's description. Had they mentioned the guy dropped from a fire escape ladder, they would've acted with greater speed. In a studdered, winded voice, they heard, "We're in foot pursuit of the suspect." A unit blocked the alleged killer at St. Ann and Dauphine. Other units responded, and the night air was like a psychedelic blue strobe fest as the unit's lights flashed. They had him trapped, and like any cornered animal, he decided to fight back, shooting one of the officers. Simultaneously, a street cop yelled, "Gun, gun, gun!" as one of the other cops fell. Then, guns started blazing at the suspect. He was toast. It would have been better had they taken him alive, but shooting one of their own, the writing was on the wall. Questions remained. Did they have all his murder victims? People rarely reported missing corner prostitutes.

Dispatch lit up as Trey's, Max', and the other four detective's radios began wildly squawking. Max stuck his head in interrogation and called to Trey, waving his hand to come to the door. In an attempted whisper, Max said, "They got him."

After the big bruhaha of intense gunfire, the Coroner's office got to the scene. The suspect, not yet a man, appeared to be in his teens. All working the site took on a look of dismay. It was shitty when the suspect was a grown-ass adult with some wires crossed, but a kid. It was hard to fathom. As the Coroner had the suspect flipped over and laid out in a body bag, a crinkled piece of blood-spattered paper fell out of his pocket. Perhaps a confession, probably not.

Mom, I'm sorry, but I couldn't take it anymore—the men, drugs and drinking. I tried to ignore it, but I couldn't any longer. Since you are reading this, then it has already happened. It would be easier to die than live with you. I've tried a few times but couldn't do it, so I posed as the City Slasher attempting a getaway. The police would easily capture me, and if I shot one of them, I wouldn't have to worry any longer; they'd take me out. I will always love you. Peter

The Coroner's assistant rubbed her forehead; she felt sick to her stomach. "Don, you gotta see this. Shit." She passed the note to the Coroner.

He took the note, and as he read it, he paced. "You gotta be kidding me. The media is gonna love this one." Don was one of those men from a rough district. Determined to get out of the housing project, he knuckled down and put himself through college and med school. He chanced into the Assistant Coroner position, and after a few years, with his boss' passing, he became the man in charge. Seeing the sickening lack of humanity and what people could do and did to each other took a particular inner strength. How could someone so young see no way out? He'd had it rough, but it made him all that more determined to escape the madness.

Trey's phone lit up. It was Max who knew he was in the middle of a shit storm. "Excuse me." He stepped out.

Max leaned against the wall, shaking his head. "Padna, we got ourselves a fuckin' mess. It was a planned suicide by cop and just some angry kid who didn't see a way out. We ain't got the Slasher, Trey, just some poor kid thinking he had the weight of the world on his shoulders. So sad. But it means our serial killer is still on the streets. The boy in interrogation?"

Trey slapped the file on his side, disgusted. "Nah, he's not the guy. I'm cutting him loose. If he were the guy, Babe wouldn't have stepped up."

Minutes later, Babe and Boyd walked out of the police department. He looked down at the kid, "Boyd, you still living at your mom's place?" The kid nodded. "Who lives there with y'all?"

Boyd cocked a smile, "No one permanent. They come and go, you know. As soon as I'm eighteen, I'm outta there and joining the Navy. I'm gonna be a Navy Seal."

Babe pondered, then asked, "You know anything about the Navy? Find out the facts before rushing into anything, but it might be the perfect fit. Being a SEAL is some tall order. " He gave him a ride and asked for his address. It was quick to drop him off. *Yep, same apartment. I wonder who is in my old place. Great fuckin' memories.* He felt a broad smile inside. Trinity, with her tight little body and their outstanding sex, was memorialized in his tiny apartment. *That was one hell of a shower.* "Ooh-rah!" He said aloud in his truck. He headed back to the house; it had been a long night, and he planned to bring Chancée to see Trinity.

Carlton stood to the side of his window, occasionally peering out. The blue-wigged whore curled in a ball. Her body shuddered with trapped gasps of air between tears. The maniac had already made it clear to keep silent, and because she hadn't at first, he gagged her with a dirty old rag. It was rank with crusty layers of spunk. Something ran across her leg, causing a muffled squeal from the gag. "Shut up, disgusting whore." He peeked out the window again. The area, infested with cops, left him to stay huddled in his tiny room. They didn't understand he was cleaning up the city one whore at a time. Nobody cared about them; they were either runaways or junkies. They had spread disease from one end of the city to the other. They'd pay for what they'd done.

It all started on his eighteenth birthday, and his three friends pitched in to pay for a whore. Their buddy was the only one of the foursome of friends that hadn't gone all the way. He was a small guy, maybe five-six, with nondescript light brown hair, eyes to match, and a pitted, acne-scarred face. None of the girls took a second look at him, even the ugly ones. The mask of acne thwarted even the possibility of attention once under a street lamp or porch light.

They rode in Bobert's dad's silver le Baron, sharing a six-pack along the way. Once they paid the hooker, they'd planned to stand guard by the car while he had his first bang. They pulled up to a block from the House of Blues. Bobert, the most experienced of the four, walked toward Canal Street. He offered the cash to the first hooker to approach him, explaining it was his friend's birthday and he was a virgin. She didn't care who was getting what but smiled anyway. Carlton sat alone in the backseat, pants pulled down with his dick harder than ever before. Bobert opened the car door, the front seat already as far forward to give the maximum space for his first fuck.

"Happy Birthday," she crooned. "I got just what you need to celebrate the occasion." She mounted him. He guided himself inside; it was glorious.

She bounced up and down. "Baby, you sure you're eighteen; I never felt such a small cock." Embarrassed, he felt a shrivel effect in progress. "She grabbed it and began pumping it back to its full child-like size. "Now, that's more like it." She hopped on board, pushing herself harder onto him, and in moments, her hard-earned effort gave him the expected and desired outcome. "For your first time, baby, you held on longer than most. Sorry for what I said. Nothing's wrong with your cock." He knew most people referred to a woody as six inches, but he thought it was all talk. His three-inch stub, he figured, was par for the course. Her comment played and re-played in his mind. He was sure the guys outside heard it, and it was mortifying. They climbed back in the car after she left.

"Carlton, she said you gave it like a pro. And? How was it?" He didn't know what to tell Bobert, but the whole thing after her comment was embarrassing. "Like you expected?"

If the guys could see his face, they'd see the bright red flush and shame. "Better." He decided he'd return after leaving the boys and seek retribution. From doing it so much, her box was probably worn and stretched. It was her, not him, with the problem.

Maybe he didn't get retribution that night, but his fantasy only lasted a few months when he implemented the plan. He'd never forget her face; she'd never shatter another young man's dreams. Carlton packed a gym bag with tape, a knife, twine, rubbers, and his old blanket from when he was a baby. He kept it hidden under his mattress. It was soft except for a few crusty areas. He added a couple of hoodies, tees, and jeans. The bag was ready if and when he mustered enough courage.

The night of graduation at the post-party, he found courage with weed and an entire six-pack. Gnawing obsession turned into a perpetual stiffy, and he was ready. She'd learn what humiliation felt like. The internet had given him ideas. If a baby could come out, then what could go in it to humiliate someone? He lifted a bottle of beer out of their fridge. Carlton had to return his father's car before two in the morning. His parents' friends had been generous with graduation cash totaling one thousand one hundred and fifty dollars—a hundred here, a fifty there, and his grandparents with their five hundred was spectacular. He stashed most of the money in his gym bag, leaving a hundred and fifty in his pocket.

Bobert parked in front of Carlton's next-door neighbor's house with his car running lights turned off, perfect for a quick getaway. Carlton took a second to get his things and stole away into the night and Bobert's running vehicle. He slid in, and they took off. "Just drop me at Canal close to Decatur. I got it from there."

Bobert winked at his friend with a big smile, "Bet I know what you're doing with your graduation money," and laughed. "You gettin' some. It's better than those lame chicks from school. You gonna rent one of those cheap ass nasty rooms; hope you're up to date on all your shots," he coughed loudly. First things first was acquiring the room. He thumped the roof as he climbed out. "Hey, Carlton, dude, make sure you get your money's worth. Don't shoot you're wad too fast," and he pulled away.

The first sign he saw that looked like it could be rent for the night, he knocked on the door. An older lady, like his mother's age, with bleach blonde hair and a gravely deep voice, answered. "Ma'am, is the room still for rent? I'll be in town for a few days. I'll pay in cash right now." One eyebrow raised sharply.

She looked him up and down. Still wearing his suit from graduation, he looked spiffed up. "Since it's cash, I'll give you a break at two-fifty per night, so how many nights?" He pulled out seven hundred and fifty from his gym bag. "I'll cut you a deal since the night is almost over." She handed him fifty back and said, "Should get you a little something, sweetie. Look for a hot pink wig. She can suck a ball through a garden hose," and winked.

The woman led the way to a dingy room on the second floor. The boards underfoot creaked, and from the sound of it, there was activity behind the other four doors along the hallway. His room came equipped with a bed, a lamp next to a well-worn padded chair, and a mirror hung on the bathroom door reflecting the over-stuffed chair. It wreaked of funk and grime. As she turned her back to him, showing him the nasty little bathroom, he came behind her with his knife, slicing her across the neck. She coughed and sputtered, reaching for him, eyes bulging in fear as she struggled with her last breaths. He stood over her body in disbelief of himself. There wasn't the slightest bit of shame or remorse. He pulled down her powder pink leggings, took a long look at her parts, and jerked himself until he was ready. It didn't take long, and he forced her legs apart, shoving himself into her. She was still warm inside. He banged with all he had, then once finished, he rolled her body tightly in the moldy shower curtain liner and tossed it out of the bathroom window into a heap of trash. She was his test run, and as far as he was concerned, he got an A plus for courage, lack of hesitation, and accuracy of the deed.

Carlton used one of the four dingy white towels to clean up the mess. He moved the chair from the wall, covering most of the blood stain by the corner of the puffy chair. Looking in the mirror, he straightened his shirt, tucking it tight into his trousers. Besides the seven hundred of his cash, the older woman had another five hundred dollars. He stashed all but two hundred, separated it in fifty-dollar increments, and utilized different pockets so his whole roll wouldn't be exposed. It was something his dad told him on one of their family vacations to the coast. 'Carlton, never pull out all your cash at one time; there are people out there that will grab it all. Keep your money hidden in different pockets.' What would his dad think of him now? His dad did everything but call him a pussy because he didn't play football, or any sport for that matter. He was a computer nerd with enough saved porn for many hours of choking the chicken.

Some of the whores had called it a night, but he saw the hot pink wig. He cautiously approached. She batted her eyelashes, "Hey, derlin', I was just about to start home. You lookin' for a late night date 'cause I could be your girl. What's your pleasure?"

"Miss, I have a room if—"

She interrupted, "You are probably staying by Lydia's place. Rooms to rent?" He nodded. "How about we walk around the block? I have the perfect hideaway corner away from prying eyes. I'll even cut you a break." She offered a blowjob for fifty or a handy for thirty. He thought *that's a no-brainer*. Her hidden spot was where there were stacks of nasty garbage bags—a trash alley. He could see a foot poking out of the shower curtain he had wrapped Lydia's body in, but Miss Hot Pink Hair was at a disadvantage. He was at the ready when she pulled up a stool she had for such occasions in her guarded hidey-hole. He pulled himself from his pants, she giggled. "Isn't that the cutest thing I've seen in a long time? I like myself a small dick; it gives me enough room in my mouth to tickle your fancy. I hate those big old Johnsons; you can hardly get your mouth around them. Ain't much fun there—no room to work." Lydia had been right, the girl had a vacuum for a mouth, and he felt like she damned near swallowed the whole thing. She finished, then looked up at him, "Don't you let no one hassle you over your package. Let them know it's because they don't know nothing about suckin' no dick." She winked at him. If anything other than pleasure, she gave him levity in his step and didn't make him feel like he was president of the teeny weenie club.

With the transaction complete, he returned to Lydia's rooms for rent. How long would it be until someone noticed her missing? The trash looked overdue for a haul. Would they see the body? He was sure they'd seen their share of strange things in the trash heaps around the city, maybe even a body or two.

With a night of deep satisfaction, he stripped his clothes, hung them in the closet, and crawled in under the sheets.

Chancée woke up with the birds, and since it wasn't a weekday, everyone, including Ruthie, slept. The grandfather clock in the living room chimed off with eight loud gongs. Eight was extremely late for Ruthie to be sleeping. He didn't want to overstep, but he needed to check on her to satisfy his mind. He walked up to her door and heard muttering and movement. The old gal was okay.

Downstairs, he prepared a bottle for the baby, rested her against his thighs, and began humming a soft lullaby.

Quietly, Ruthie descended the stairs and, in a whisper, said, "You know, your grandfather had a lovely voice. Boy, you take after him in so many ways. Your little girl is fortunate to have a loving and kind father." She put the coffee to drip. "I'm sorry I slept so late, but your princess was up half the night. When you came in, I believe it was five this morning; I had just gotten her back to sleep. Babe, she knows when you're home and when you're not." She raised an eyebrow.

He gazed at Ruthie, snickering and knowing what she probably thought. He wanted to say, nope, he wasn't banging anyone, but let her to her thoughts. She turned the television on to the news. The story unfolded about the serial killer, the boy they thought was the suspect, and there he was, big as day, exiting the police department with the wrongfully held boy. Her mouth dropped agape; she looked back and forth from the television to him. Her eyebrows drew together like she was about to ask him why he said nothing. With a chuckle, he said, "Ruthie, I've learned you are a woman who will think what you want until otherwise proven wrong. Not that you are wrong very often, but I know you thought I was meeting Javier and a couple," he cleared his throat, "escorts." His body tingled from remembering the excitement of hearing Trinity's voice. The electrified nerves were just under the skin, causing a tickle in his heart. *What is it with these emotions?* He tipped the bottle, assuring no air bubbles.

"I spent a good bit of time at the hospital with Trinity." His smile beamed. He felt his face flush and knew the tips of his ears were most likely beet red. *Miracles, thank you, God.* "She said my name." *Another unswallowable lump. Fuck. What's next, fucking tears?* "We communicated, having one-word answers. Ruthie, we had better enjoy it while it lasts because we know my wife can talk a long mile. When the police brought the boy in, his one phone call was to Trinity's uncle, who told him to tell the police to call me. I better brush up on the law if people are gonna start calling me for representation." He started to burp Chancée, "Can you get a burp cloth and pack up her diaper bag? She's going to see her mom this morning".

BIG PLANS

The traffic was unusually light on St. Charles Avenue. It was tranquil, with just the right amount of sun filtering through the oak branches lining the avenue. Babe could see her little face reflecting off her car seat mirror. From her mirror to his rearview, her eyes locked on his. He'd glance up every other moment. No doubt, she was his girl. "Chancée, you have stolen my heart. I can't wait for your mom to set eyes on you. You are a special gift." Just as Babe was pulling in, she announced she'd had enough of the car seat and wailed an ear and spine-piercing cry. "Wow, girl, you 'bout deafened me, and here I was thinking how peaceful and serene our time together was. Fuck that notion. No, no, dammit, no cursing in front of the baby," he scolded himself. "I'm coming; hold tight." The squalling didn't cease until he popped the seat out of his truck. As quick as the piercing torturous sound started, it ended. She'd gotten her way and was out of the vehicle.

The security guard nodded as he entered, and of course, he smiled when he saw the carrier. Babe thought, *I better get used to this; it'll be a lifetime of strangers ogling over my girl.* His heart fluttered with excitement; he couldn't wait for Trinity to hold their baby. She hadn't seen the baby from everybody's account, but he didn't trust any of them in the jigsaw puzzle of reality. It was perplexing how easily Antoine and Antoinette tried to deceive him. After the dust settled, he'd address the situation and web of lies. Whose idea was it? Who knew? What would Trinity's take be? Babe was a man of his word; thus, he'd nixed any follow-up on re-enlisting; he more or less had given Antoine his word.

Like a gaggle of geese, the nurses and aides bustled around Babe and the carrier. Babbling about the beautiful baby and how much she looked like him, he could hardly get a word in. Finally, he cleared his throat loudly and asked, "How is my wife today? Any more progress, or is she still communicating with one word?" He huffed a snicker, "Under normal circumstances, my wife is verbose and high energy like a pinwheel on a gusty day."

Her nurse quickly responded that she had hardly said a word, more nods or shrugs. His heart dropped. Is that how it was going to be? Good one day and not so much the next? The thought was reminiscent of his grandfather, but the difference was cognition between morning and night, not day to day. The nursing community called it Sundowners. He swallowed hard, pasting a smile on his face, and knocked. "Trinity, it's Babe."

"C'mon in, big guy." As he pushed the privacy curtain to the side, she saw the carrier inciting a waterfall of tears. She put out her hands, curling her fingers in a pulse-like motion. "My baby." Babe took Chancée out of the carrier and placed the baby in her arms. She kissed her forehead and each tiny finger. "So beautiful, Babe."

He pulled up a chair, resting his chin on his fist, watching his two loves. "Girl, we made a pretty baby. I think we're like yin and yang, or whatever the fuck the expression is." He watched Trinity's fascination with her baby. Noticing the missing urine bag, he cautiously asked, "Have you gotten up?" She smiled and nodded. "Can you walk?" She shook her head, sadly closing her eyes. "That's okay; you've made unbelievable strides, my lady. Time." She weakly smiled. "One day at a time, girl."

She shrugged as a tear trickled down her cheek. "Maybe." She waited a few seconds, then said, "Maybe not."

Trinity played with the baby, and when it was time to change her diaper, she was lightning fast, getting the wet one off and the clean one on. Babe commented on how speedy she was and how bumbling he'd felt initially. "Nieces, nephews," she replied with a half-smile. Trinity laid Chancée on her chest, gently rubbing her back with whisper-like kisses on the crown of her head. Babe rested his hand on her thigh. It was disconcerting; he knew if he tightened his grip to capacity, it felt like her femur would snap. Physical therapists had their work cut out to get her back to her usual strength and agility. He whispered, I love you, not wanting to disturb their slumber-like tranquility. Her eyes opened to barely slits as she returned the sentiment. "Babe, I love you." Three little words, but words that filled his heart. Those were the words he'd longed to hear.

There was a light tap on the door; he jumped up quickly. It was his in-laws. Could he be civil? Did he even want to speak to them? For Trinity's sake, he would not create turmoil or stress. Her mom teared up, seeing Trinity with the baby. Babe, still standing, offered the chair to her mother and then stood against the wall, hands clasped behind him. He could feel Antoine looking at him. *Ignore or drill right back? Civility*. He acquiesced and turned his head with a slight twitch of a smile. Antoine tipped his head to the side, indicating that he wanted to talk to Babe out of Trinity's earshot. The Marines trained him to control anger with intellect, and he'd need to dig deep; he knew he could do it. Rattling around in his head were some of Antoine's last words imparted by the elevator. *If I wanted you dead, you'd be dead.*

They stepped outside. "The last time we spoke, Marine, was an emotional time. I said things I shouldn't have." Babe supposed such was the closest thing the man could verbalize as an apology. "We are not out of the woods, but appearances indicate she's on the mend." He acknowledged her father with a brief nod. "Are you willing to wait?" *What the fuck?*

"Sir, when I made my vows to Trinity at our wedding, I meant them. I can't believe you're asking me such a question." He could feel the heat rising from his gut up to his throat. "I know it will be a long road, but I'm here for the fair and foul weather. I have one question: who decided to use Angelette as an impostor? You or your wife? Did you actually think I wouldn't know? I was grief-stricken and knew of instances when people had personality changes. And maybe because I wanted to believe, I allowed myself to jump into the web of lies, but I knew. Hell, my dog, housekeeper, and boys knew. So who?"

Antoine answered it was Bethany at first, but seeing such a similar image to Trinity filled the void in their hearts even though they knew the ruse. We all know it was a huge mistake."

"Ya think?" The sarcasm was thick.

He asked about the rumor of Babe re-enlisting. The answer was easy; he'd given his word, and he lived by his word. So, no. He was, however, going to help the NOPD find the serial killer known as The Slasher. Antoine raised an eyebrow, wondering why he would do that. Simple, it was the right thing to do. His father-in-law shrugged, mentioning that intelligent people only put themselves out there for family. Why risk dying for a stranger?

"Trinity knows that is who I am and is down with it. Some people run away from a burning building, and others run to the blaze. I'm one of those that run to it, and for your information, I'm no stooge."

Antoinette came out the door saying Trinity was looking for Babe. He bid farewell and went back into the room with his wife.

He returned to the chair after kissing her. "Your visit with your mother went well?"

She half-smiled, "Yes. She talked."

"Do you remember me telling you about Angelette, your cousin?" She nodded and said sorry. "I know it was an emotional time, but your parents crossed a line. We've all kissed and made up, not literally," he chuckled. "On a serious note, there's a serial killer in the Quarter raping and killing working girls. I'm gonna help catch his ass. I'm telling you because I might not be able to stay as long when I visit, but I will see you every day, ma girl. Is it okay if Ruthie and the boys visit?" She smiled even brighter. "I need to take the princess home, and you need your rest. Work hard with PT." He took Chancée, put her in the carrier, and leaned in for a quick peck. Trinity grabbed the back of his neck and forced a deeper kiss. "I love you, ma girl, and the sooner you get better, the sooner you can come home."

The police presence was heavy in the Quarter, but business had to return to normal. They missed their chance at finding the serial killer before, but Babe was determined to catch the bastard. New Orleans was his city, and no stupid motherfucking degenerate was going to put another mark on his city. After dropping the baby home with Ruthie, he headed to the Quarter, parked by his old apartment, and began weaving through the blocks on foot.

Creating follies in his mind, Carlton nearly bumped into several people. They'd just think he was drunk. Then, he saw an incredible opportunity. Across the street, a prim and proper grandmother-like woman struggled to bring a flower pot from her front door into the house. It was the perfect situation to find a place to lay low. She held one pot.

"Ma'am, I'll get the other one for you. I'm Carlton." He projected his sweet-as-pie smile.

"What a lovely young man. Thank you."

He followed her to the kitchen in the back of the house. Quickly drawing out the knife, he cut her throat. She was thin and fragile; the knife nearly cut to her vertebrae. He laid three big lawn and leaf bags on the living room floor after rolling up her Oriental rug. They were the kind that were thicker than usual for branches or soil. Carlton dragged her body onto the plastic and decided since her head was almost detached anyway, he'd finish the job. Once finished, he sat looking at the head. He liked to fuck the whores right after he killed them because their body was still warm and moist, no noise, no fighting, but the thought of the older woman repulsed him.

He wedged open her lifeless eyes, knelt in front of the head, and jerked off while he talked trash. He had to get off; this score was fantastic, severing a head. He played a loop of the jocks who teased and bullied him. He pictured them watching him in horror as he unloaded his wad into the condom. It would have felt much better if it had been all over her face, but that would leave evidence. "Y'all want a piece of me now," he spoke to the imaginary crowd of athletes and popular kids. "Doctor Pimple Popper? How about Mr. Getting Ahead?" Carlton laughed out loud. No more nerd Carlton, pussy douchebag, or pizza face. He savored the moment.

Wondering what other garden tools she might have, he went to the backyard shed. She had a man-size shovel that could mix cement and a hoe. He'd seen his father use a hoe after they uprooted some bush. The edge seemed sharp, not like a knife, but a hard edge, which sparked an idea. He grabbed another lawn and leaf bag and went into the living room. He raised the hoe over his head and swung down, creating a big gash in her right wrist. After a few more swings, the hand detached. He moved around her body, severing all the joints. Some were much harder to separate, and he worked up a sweat, creating big rings under the arms of his shirt.

Once he'd finished mutilating her entire body, he put the pieces in the bag and wrapped her torso like a gift with the three bags under her body, using the tape from his bag. He carried her wrapped torso in search of a garbage can. He ultimately found them down the side of the house. Both were atop a layer of bricks. Stacks of bricks on the side of either garbage cans gave stability. Getting the package into the garbage can was more difficult than imagined, and it turned over, knocking down a brick mini wall and causing a ruckus with the clamoring sounds of metal cans. Carlton didn't see the hand come over the top of the gate but noticed when a person started to enter. He grabbed her arm and pulled as the gate caught her red shoe, leaving her only one shoe.

"Who are you?" The girl demanded. "Where's Mrs. Lila Rose? Are you her nephew?" He held her close, pinned her to his body, and quickly grabbed a brick before she screamed. Her eyes bulged in fear, knowing this was no friend, then the lights went out as he smashed her skull. She was out cold. He took her unconscious body, dropped it on one of the bushes encircling the garden fountain, stretched her head back, and cut her from ear to ear. Blood sprayed onto his shirt.

"You useless whore, you want to dirty me, well—" he struggled to get her bottoms off, then pushed himself inside of her. "Now I'm gonna make you dirty, you whore." His voice was like a low growl.

After finishing with the girl, he ensured the garbage cans were back in place and returned to the house. The body parts were all in the bag; the only thing left was the woman's head, which he brought to the shed and dropped in one of the flower pots in the dark rear corner. Back inside the house, he tried to straighten the rug and furniture to appear undisturbed and mopped the mess in the kitchen with paper towels. It would be a perfect place to hide. No one would be looking for her, but once someone discovered the hooker's body, he'd have to return to the rooms to rent shithole. First, he found the washer and dryer, sprayed stain remover on the blood, and added bleach. Carlton had seen his mother do that when he split his lip on the front steps and bled on his tee shirt. Lastly, the detergent and the waiting game until the cycle finished.

While waiting, he checked the refrigerator and found various things to make a filling ham sandwich. He watched TV, ate his sandwich, and waited for his shirt. On the screen was a live alert as the forensic team pulled a body from the back of a truck. A gorgeous girl with thick, bouncy, black hair stood to the side so the camera crew could get her and the garbage truck in the coverage.

"Locals are on heightened alert with yet another kill from The City Slasher. The slain bodies are increasing daily, and now, with a heavy heart, the discovery of his latest victim, Ms. Lydia Scott, has sent shock waves through the community. She's been a welcoming home to many a traveler or lost soul, providing rooms to rent for a nominal fee." Carlton spoke back to the television, saying nominal was far from the truth. "Neighbors and friends will miss Lydia's colorful character and good heart. This is

Alexa—" He turned to another channel for more urgent news about the has-been whore, Lydia.

Exasperated, he checked his shirt; there were about ten minutes until the cycle finished. He returned to the kitchen, looking for snacks. The mail slot squeaked open; he ducked around the corner. The mirror reflected a pair of brown eyes looking through the slot, trying to peer to the far right and left. "Mrs. Lila, it's Colette; I dropped your mail. Have yourself a nice day." The mail slot clanked close. His body trembled uncontrollably. Had he still been watching TV, the mail carrier would have spotted him. Now, with the news about Lydia, he wondered if his room would be off-limits. He'd left his phone charger, a monumental mistake, and the chair barely covered her blood-stained rug. His fingerprints were all over the room, but he was sure there would be a million others. If the police were observant, they'd notice a missing shower liner. As far as he knew, she didn't keep a paper trail of occupants.

After passing a few blocks without any peculiarities, Babe prowled even more, heightening his senses like a lion in the wild. He spotted a single worn red patent leather pump resting against a residential gate. The big guy knew it was trespassing, but his curiosity was piqued. He reached over and quickly maneuvered the latch. There was a lock, but it was for show. He passed two garbage cans on the narrow path, noting a littering of bricks sitting next to asymmetrical brick walls. He kept going. Babe noted no security lights, no big dog, and nothing for protection from intruders. The place was void of activity; the only sound was a rhythmic spatter from a fountain. Slumped in the bushes around the fountain was the body of a young woman. She was missing a shoe and was naked from the waist down.

Once again, the perpetrator had cut her throat, only this time, it was almost down to the bone. As was his M.O., the killer positioned her hand to his exit, but it was pointing toward a small garden shed. *Take the bait or call it in?* Curiosity got the best of him, and he opened the door, expecting an attack. All he found were a potter's bench and a sundry of home gardening supplies. He started to turn around and return to the garden when he saw an object in one of the empty planters. *Fuck me.* There was a severed head in the flower pot. So, the pointed hand wasn't a way out; it was proof of sick mastery. It was a game to the killer, like cat and mouse.

He texted Trey: Call me. Another body

His phone immediately buzzed. Trey started the usual questions. "Where? Where you at?" Babe unraveled the story. It didn't take long for Max and the Crime Lab to arrive.

"So why point to the shed?" He asked.

Babe said those were his exact thoughts and knew a fight would be on once the door opened, but it wasn't. "Go take a look." A string of cursing rang from the small shed. Max left the door open and instructed the team about the severed head. The older detective's face blanched; he looked like he was going to be sick. "So Max, you got a headless body somewhere unless he got creative and left a meat puzzle—an arm here, a leg there."

He pulled a rumpled handkerchief from his pocket and dabbed the sweat on his brow. "Why you do me dat? Babe, you're twisted. Was that your first thought, pal? Sick. I gotta get the place locked down. Ya know, what choo did was trespassin', maybe even breaking and entering the shed? Possible but not probable." A uniform showed up on the scene. Max tossed the yellow crime scene tape to him and told him to lock it down. "Babe, you can't be here no more."

The case jumped up a few notches; not that a string of dead prostitutes wasn't already horrific, but now it was unquestionable the guy was playing with them.

Trey's voice bellowed from the side of the house, "Anyone call the owner, or do we even know who the owner is?"

Babe thought perhaps the owner's head was in the flower pot. He didn't verbalize his gut. They discovered from a neighbor that the owner was Lila Rose, a kind elderly woman. Trey was on the phone with his captain. She wasn't in their system, and the captain had already gotten a search warrant. He was coming to the scene. "Let me know what you find out if you can, Max." The Marine hustled out of there and continued on the street. He'd wind up and down every street. Like an ever-changing montage, ideas of what they would find in the house ticked over in his mind. Dollars to donuts, the head belonged to the owner of the house. So far, it had only been working girls, and now, it was an elderly lady and a younger woman who didn't have the appearance of an escort, but maybe. Did he kill them, then do them, so there was no fight or screaming, minimizing his chance of getting caught?

Babe started internalizing: how would I select my prey? Crimes committed in plain sight get accomplished, for the most part. Perfect prey musts: single or with a tight, big crowd, but then again, his method of killing wasn't bloody. No, this killer had to have his victim alone in a private location. Maybe he had a place in the Quarter, probably close to where the girls would strut their stuff. Three places came to mind. The problem was anyone could be the predator: rich, poor, young, old, scuzzy, well-kempt, black, white, a local guy or traveler, and there was always a married, church-going family man or single hustler. He left that evening with more questions and fewer answers.

Babe got his morning workout completed. Ruthie had mentioned she and the boys were going to visit Trinity and was insistent they wouldn't stay long or tire her. He planned that while they were visiting, he'd start collecting facts and see if the police or he missed any glaring inaccuracies.

One foot in front of the other, he went down one street, up another, and wove his tracks like weaving a fine basket. He needed a reference chart. First, he'd list all the victims; then, were the girls killed at night or during the day? Where did they turn their tricks or pick up johns? His reconnaissance training and years of practice would come in handy.

He turned, crossed over, went a block, and started up another street. He completed Rampart Street, and only four ladies had approached him so far, but then again, it was morning. After going a block on Canal, he turned onto Burgundy, where he noticed people hustling to Canal to catch a bus or ones that had recently gotten off. The groups of teens emerged from the bus like ants from a pile. They seemed mesmerized by their phones and oblivious to anything else around them. One block up was Iberville, and tempted as he was to turn down, he kept moving forward on Burgundy toward Esplanade.

Five working girls huddled, listening to what he assumed was their pimp. He heard the man tell the girls it was getting real and that Lydia had gone missing, but the garbage truck crew found her amidst a pickup. *Mental note: Who's Lydia?* He kept moving at a significant pace. Babe went into an establishment and straight to their second-floor balcony. He scanned the street, and nothing appeared out of the ordinary. It was unusually quiet for that part of the Quarter, given it was morning. The area wasn't particularly ideal for the working girl, but he'd seen the five, so maybe he was wrong. Perhaps given the heightened alert, the pimp brought them together. Things were fucked up.

After hours of recon, he called it quits and made a course to his truck. Midway down the block, he ran into a wall of putridity. He knew there was a decaying dead body close by—human or animal was anybody's guess. Trey always looked at Babe with an eye of suspicion, whereas Max was far more approachable. If he called Trey, he'd have to hear about Babe and his coincidental finding of bodies or tragedies. Babe deferred to Max and told him about a potential rotting corpse. He said he wasn't hanging around; he was off to see Trinity. His directions were sound; the older detective wouldn't have trouble finding the area. Crossing the street at a good clip, he came close to mowing down a pimply-faced teenage boy in a suit of all things. The young man looked too adolescent for job hunting; he didn't fit in as a kid skipping school. The suit waved a red flag and sent Babe's feels on edge.

THE IMPOSTOR LIE

Standing on the corner in thigh-high black boots, a skimpy skirt, and a sequined top was the working girl he'd given a ride to after the Chop debacle. Instead of a blunt-cut pink wig, she had cascading waist-length mahogany curls. She flashed a smile and, in a flirty tone, told him it'd been a long time since she'd seen him and asked if he was still hanging with the Latino girl. Babe held up his left hand, showing the wedding band. "Good for you, Marine, but remember, pay to play is always hush-hush with no strings attached." He winked at her and said perhaps he'd keep it in mind. *Fat fucking chance of that,* he snickered. A thought came to mind in a blink, and he turned around. He asked if she knew Lydia. "Dawlin', everyone knows her. She runs a room to rent in a place close to Decatur and Canal. She says it's rent by the day, but if business is slow, she'd rent by the hour. There's a big fucking sign. In her day, Lydia was a hot piece of ass, so the story goes. Why?" Babe answered, just curious he'd heard the name. He also warned her to be careful. She patted her pocket and whispered Mace spray. Once again, he was on the way to his truck and Trinity.

Almost like a strobing sign, the pimply-faced kid kept niggling his mind. The boy carried a small duffle bag, and it looked like he was tweaking, but he wasn't. He was a category unto himself, which got under Babe's skin. With a head full of memories of his girl, he made it to his truck and was on his way down St. Charles Avenue. Heat rose in his body, creating a hot, hard poker in his pants. *Great,* he thought.

When he arrived at the hospital, Babe had to make the block looking for a parking place. He ended up a couple of blocks away. Cracking a smile, he thought about the kid who tried to rob him. The world was going mad. Babe didn't see the old Mercedes and figured Ruthie, Chancée, and the boys had finished their visit, nor did he notice Antoine or Antoinette's vehicles. Hopefully, he would have his wife to himself. He checked the login sheet. Yes, Ruthie and company had come and gone, as had her parents. The security guard welcomed him and said all her visitors had finished visiting except one man. He scanned the sheet but didn't recognize any names. Curiosity took a bite into him. The stairs would be far faster than the elevator.

In no time flat, he was outside her room. He tapped on the glass as he slid the door open. Javier was in the chair, one leg crossed over the other. He looked as sophisticated as he always did. Babe went to the far side of the bed and kissed Trinity. "Hey, you," she said. "Javier and I have been chatting." Her cognitive functions were returning at an impressive rate.

Babe walked around and shook Javier's hand. "So, you been talking with my wife, have you? I hope you were polite." He looked at Trinity and winked, then back at Javier, "Thoughts, sir?"

Javier chuckled, "You hit the lottery with this one. What she sees in you is a mystery. She regaled what she remembered of the attack, but after hearing about all her injuries, she excelled in recovery. You were correct, Marine; she is a rare beauty." Trinity smiled and touched Babe's hand.

With starlights twinkling in her eyes, she looked at Babe and cooed, "He is handsome and my superhero." She batted her eyes slowly. She looked tired. It was no wonder with the barrage of visitors she had entertained.

"Superhero?" Javier chuckled. "She needs her rest. Will I see you at the house later?" He questioned Babe, who nodded. Then he took Trinity's hand and kissed the top of it. "Speedy recovery, hermosa dama. I will stop in and say goodbye before leaving town. I meant what I said; you and your family have an open invitation to Barcelona." He shook Babe's hand. "Later, my friend."

Babe pulled the chair as close to the bed as possible, saying he wanted to hear about her day. "Can you tell me about your day instead? Mine is lying here, visitors coming to gawk at me, physical therapy, which is discouraging, and disgusting food. On a bright note, I saw the boys and Chancée. Ruthie has them in line. That's my day; yours is bound to be more exciting."

Babe relaxed, no longer sitting like a stiff board. He stroked her hand

and looked like he was at peace, a most unusual expression. His eyes softened, gazing at her. He unraveled the story of the boy in the suit. He went back over the slasher and the string of murders. He told her about mapping out the quarter, trying to narrow the search for the killer. Babe felt in his bones that the teenage boy had something to do with it—no particular reason, just a gut feeling when he passed him. He put off a weird vibe and likened it to magnets, with a north and south pole or positive and negative. Opposite poles attract and come together, like people, but identical personalities repelled. That's why they worked so well together. She was chatty; he was quiet. He added one step further to illustrate she was fun and energetic while he was still and contemplative.

Babe stressed, "The kid in the suit has a similar charge to me, making him highly suspect. Next time I see him, I'm gonna follow him and find out where his lair is. I think he has five, maybe six murders, all having to do with working girls, except for an elderly woman, which is perplexing. Maybe his mother worked the streets, or somehow, a streetwalker mocked him. The ladies have always been good to me, but I've heard of other men who didn't have the same experience. You know, the kind of things that disheartens certain men." She looked curious, not understanding. "Ya know, premature ejaculation, mysterious shrinking dick, or unable to get off, not forgetting comments about size—too big, too small, pencil-thin or bulbous. Not all penises are alike, not that I'm an authority on anyone else's pecker but mine, and sometimes even it has a will of its own." He grinned.

Trinity looked like she wanted to say something but wouldn't get it off the starting block. He asked point-blank what did she want to know. It was about Angelette; couldn't he tell the difference between her and her cousin? She said she didn't want details, but—

"Girl, you are smokin', and no one, in all my life, has set me ablaze like you. Her eyes looked different, duh, because of contacts; as far as intimacy, she sparked but didn't blaze. You, ma girl, are the only one I have eyes for. I desperately wanted to believe you were fine, but sorry, I don't like your cousin, and it hurt thinking that was who you became." He could still see more questions in her eyes but wouldn't press the issue. Trinity would talk in her time. Babe couldn't imagine her telling him she'd had sex with another man because she missed him.

Someone from P.T. knocked and entered with a wheelchair. "It's that time again, Sleeping Beauty." Looking at Babe, he commented, "And you must be Prince Charming. Since you are here, I'll let you put her in the chariot unless you want me to do the honors." Babe stood, saying he'd gladly accept the assignment.

Trying to keep a pan face and not have a look of shock, he stared into her eyes as the aide drew down the sheets. Babe leaned in and secured her in his arms. She held his neck, but her lower body was dead weight. He had held her many times before, but the loss of her mass was startling. When he put her in the chair, he realized her legs were not working. It took all his strength and a hard press of his tongue on his palate to keep his emotions in check. Did her parents know? Why hadn't they told him? Shock was one helluva way to find out. The aide strapped her in the chair and tried to put her feet on the metal supports. "I can do it," she fussed. The aide put his hands up in surrender and let her settle herself.

Once settled, Babe followed as the aide, a muscular Hispanic man probably in his early forties, pushed her into the elevator and down to the first floor. Opposite the front entrance was a closed wooden door with a coded lock. Once the man tapped the code, the door swung open. The equipment was similar to what the VA had for wounded warriors. Trinity rolled herself to the free-weight area. She grabbed two ten-pound weights and performed several exercises to increase her upper body strength. After working out her arms, they strapped braces to her legs, a wide belt around her waist, and lifted her from the chair between parallel bars. Her arms trembled as they strained. "Trinity, you don't need to rely on your arms; let's use those sleepy legs of yours," her physical therapist coached. Slowly, she took one step, followed by another, until she reached the end where he had her chair.

"No, dammit." She tried to turn around with decreased mobility and almost tumbled to the mat.

Babe caught her but held her where she landed into his arms. "C'mon, ma girl, push through it. You can do it. I'm here, and I gotcha but you don't need me." She inhaled deeply and pushed and pulled until she was upright. He winked at her, "Now let me see you strut your stuff." She moved slowly, one step at a time. He could see the exhaustion on her face when she arrived at the end. The therapist oozed congratulatory compliments to her, saying turning was a big deal and she'd made enormous progress. Babe masked his sadness with a heart-filled smile and a wink. "My lady, before long, you'll be dancing at Louie's, making the older gentlemen wish they were young again." She laughed; it was weak, but it was a laugh nonetheless. Whether it was the accomplishment or laughter, she had a noticeable increase in confidence.

BLEAK SOUL

*L*ydia's place was off limits, and now the police swarmed Lila Rose's bungalow like bugs to a light. There was nowhere he could go. He should have had a more decisive plan. So what if he had a little pecker; it didn't matter the cute prostitute even told him not to get hung up on the size of his johnson. The load he shot looking at Lila Rose's head was massive; it didn't matter if his dick was twelve inches or three. He might have had four when he pushed all the skin back as far as it would go. He'd gotten more sex in his escapade than any of his friends, and his conquests were pros at no cost, complete with telling tales, giving descriptions, and utter silence. Thinking about the murders sent shock waves of urgency to his penis nub. There was nothing more thrilling than being in total control of a situation. In his mind, he doubted any of his friends could kill someone. In his warped mental state, he viewed it as courage.

No doubt, the crime lab would find blood in Lydia's; the police had identified her and probably lifted every fingerprint in the room. Carlton stood in front of a store window encased with decorative metal burglar bars. He studied his reflection, noticing a straighter posture, proud of his accomplishments, but nothing screamed he was The City Slasher. He knew he was smart and figured he had outwitted the detectives on the slasher case.

He straightened his shirt and began searching for another room for rent sign. His mind drummed up other murderous methods. The ideas raced through in a whirlwind. So ensconced with the thought train, he failed to notice the massive man across the street. His mind continued to ramble. There had to be a plan to capture the whores. He had to plan it out; most were stronger and way wiser at fighting than he was.

Babe was on another fast track of thoughts. He followed the kid. What to do with the little shit? Should he turn him in or demonstrate the true nature of a predator? With the boy's juvenile face, there was no way he struck horror with his victims, maybe surprise, but not where their blood ran cold, and fear silenced their tongues. The big man naturally had those qualities, or were they curses?

The boy stopped at the door with an overhead sign advertising rooms to rent at an hourly or day rate. He noticed the kid compose his stance as he knocked. A man in an animal print wife-beater and spandex black pants answered the door. There was very little to the imagination as far as his body. The man cocked his side, placing his hand on the bony prominence of his hip.

Carlton put on his sweetest smile. "Sir, I am new in town and wanted to know if you had a room to rent. I'll be in town for a few days." He was the picture of innocence.

"You looking for a place to sleep or a place to work? Baby, I'm sorry to disappoint; you don't have what it takes to work here. If it's a place to sleep, I recommend Estelle's Board Room, which is a few blocks down, dearie. All my boys are pretty, and I only have a couple of ladies. Tell Estie that Patrick recommended her to you. Ta-Ta." He shut the door. Babe got a chuckle watching the youngster gauge the character of the man who answered the door. The boy clearly didn't butter both sides of the bread. Carlton bounced back from the rejection, knowing there was no way he could pay the man back for the insult.

Estelle's was two blocks down. He rang the doorbell. A bosomy redhead dressed in a flowing dress of sorts answered. The boy gave the same spiel as before, emphasizing he only needed a place to sleep and bathe. They discussed rental fees, and the drippy kid pulled out a roll of money. Babe thought, *you do that at night, and someone's gonna grab your roll and haul ass*. Estelle invited the boy inside. Part of him wanted to call Max, but all he could say was he had a gut feeling. No, he'd have to catch him in the act.

On the corner, he spied a hole in the wall deli. It brought memories of the place around the corner from work and what a huge disappointment it was; nonetheless, it was food. Pastrami on rye was the day's special. The sandwich, bag of chips, and soft drink came to fifteen dollars. *What a rip*.

He texted Trinity.

Babe: You good? Behaving? He chuckled to himself.

Trinity: Boy, am I. Behaving? Hmm.

Babe: What does, boy, am I mean?

Trinity: The new aide that came on makes this girl want her man. Where you at?

Javier: Popped in to say goodbye. Wow, your girl gives…He added a head with a smile.

Babe: Fuck you. You only wish. Think I might have the City Slasher. Gotta wait it out

Javier: Takes one to know one?

Babe: Sorry to see you leave. Give my wife back her phone.

Trinity: It's me. You two are like high school boys. Find the bastard, Babe. Love you.

Babe: I love you more!

It was these alone times when he missed her so deeply it made his heart ache. If they were sitting at the deli table, they could have sat for hours chatting away, more like her chatting and him captured by her words. He missed her, Chancée, the boys, and Gunner. Why did he need to catch the guy? It wasn't his job, but he felt called. *Fuck this call shit. I'm done.* Babe started to get up when the boy exited Estelle's. He still carried the canvas bag, but it wasn't bulging full as earlier. Babe kept sight of him and watched him enter a hotel. Keeping pace behind him, he, too, entered the hotel.

A tour group assembled at the other entrance; the boy shuffled among the guests, and Babe lost him. Thinking of working girl hangouts, Babe remembered one a block over from the other side of the hotel. He made it back through the door he'd entered, then double-timed it around the block and made his way to the corner where the girls would provocatively flirt, waiting for a possible client. It was still early, but they were out in force. A car pulled over; he heard the girl tell the man it was his lucky chance; the hourly special was two girls for the price of one. *Smart.*

Babe spotted the brown suit over a block almost to Jackson Square. He had one girl, the one he remembered from the Chop debacle. She had a distinctive roll to her hips when she walked; it was definitely her. She was back to the short-cropped wig, only it was angelic blue this time. If the killer managed to get her to the French Market, Babe would have little opportunity to help or catch him. It was a zoo with vendors closing for the night and shoppers racing to beat the close. There were possibilities out the ass. If he lost visuals, the big guy would need luck on his side to pick which way to go. He lost sight of him when they passed the strawberry table. It became organized chaos as the vendors broke down for the evening. An onslaught of worker bees loaded their wares, and he must have threaded through the hive.

Walking along the back of the market was like being blind. Babe was reasonably certain that the boy didn't know the massive man had followed him. On a hunch, either he was going to kill her behind the market or take her to Estelle's. There were a plethora of dark corners between the rooms for rent and the French Market, and so far, it didn't seem like the boy was too picky. Babe headed the shortest route he knew to Estelle's and waited. Twenty minutes passed, and he struck it rich; he got a visual of the boy without the girl. *Fuck.* As Carlton got closer, it was apparent she'd given him a fight as his nose was bloody, trickling down his face onto his white shirt. From his body movements, it looked like the boy was crying. Hopefully, she came out on top.

Babe's phone buzzed. Notification alert:
Trey: Call me, it's a 911

Babe called. "Where you at?" Trey wanted to know.
"In the Quarter but heading soon to Trinity," Babe replied.
"Yeah, well, son, can you stop by here? I got a working girl who says she knows you and has info on The Slasher, but wants you here. You coming?" Trey asked.
"Yes, sir, I'll stop by for a minute, tell her. What info she has is solid, I want to hear how she got away. I didn't see it go down, but I saw enough, and I know where the dude's at right this second." He wanted to ask if Trey wanted him to go in and beat the living shit out of the guy, but he knew the answer and didn't need to ask.

As Babe approached Trey's desk, the girl saw him and ran toward him, throwing her arms around the big guy. "Oh, my Gawd, Marine, the killer almost got me. He's a fucking boy and an ugly one at that, like king of the nerds. He tried to take me behind the French Market, but I knew better. He grabbed my arm; I'll probably have his dirty fingerprint bruises on my arm. He's got his dick outside of his pants; it was like peeking out; he don't got much. The son of a bitch tells me to get on my knees. I told him to fuck off and grabbed a board from a broken fruit crate and smacked him across the face with everything I had, and ran back into the market screaming. JoJo, one of the old timers takes me and calls the police. I was some scared. I don't know where the freak went, and I wasn't gonna look for him for damn sure. I know what he looks like, though."

Her clutch was tight on him; he had to peel her off his body. "Smart girl," he said, patting her back. "I know where he is right now or did fifteen minutes ago. He's renting a room at Estelle's Board Room. Rent it by the hour or night. I'll be happy to grab that little fuck and beat the pulp out of him."

Trey settled him and said he couldn't let Babe do that, or he'd end up arrested. He called a sketch artist to get her description of the killer. The big guy wished everyone a good night and went to Trinity.

Without taking off running, Carlton sped up and ducked down darkened corners, making his way to Estelle's. "Bitch, fucking whore. I'll get her next time, and it won't be a slice across the throat; she'll pay for her insolence. She doesn't know who she's playing with." His anger turned into sobs. She broke his perfect record. He unlocked the door and entered the building. On his way to his room, a prostitute had just left her john and was counting her money; consequently, she was inattentive, which posed a promising adventure.

Carlton acted as if he'd breeze past her but grabbed her by the throat and backed her into his room. "Jesus, all you had to do was ask, honey. What's your pleasure, sweetheart?" She winked at him with a devilish smile.

He took off his jacket, "My pleasure is for you to take off your clothes, lay on my bed, and spread your legs. After I do you, then it's up to you to get me going again. After that, we will move to part three of the four-course meal." He gave her six hundred dollars.

She batted her eyes, "For this, sugar, you get the whole kit and kaboodle." She ran her tongue across her lips. She started to undress while he went and cleaned the blood off his face. It was odd that she hadn't asked about the blood. He had plans for her, which would be equally as heinous as Lila Rose but with a different spin.

When he entered the room, she had complied with his instructions and was ready for the taking. He stripped off his clothes; she held the giggle upon seeing his stub-like cock, but he could tell she wanted to laugh or say something. He closed the deal on courses one and two. He filled the bathtub and said he wanted them to bathe each other. Carlton had his knife wedged behind his toiletries. "What's the nastiest thing you've ever had to do?" he asked her. Nothing came to mind; she said it was all a gift of the body at a price. "So you'll stick your tongue anywhere?"

Reluctantly, not knowing what he wanted, she said she would and probably had. He stuck three fingers inside of her, slid them in and out, and then held them an inch away from her lips. "Lick them, don't suck them, lick them and close your eyes. Slide your tongue between my fingers." The guy was weird, but it's not like she hadn't done way kinkier stuff than that. He was just a kid; what did he know? As she wriggled her tongue through his fingers, he clamped his fingers, holding her tongue, then slipped the knife into his hand and cut off her tongue in one fell swoop. Blood ran like a waterfall down her chin into the water. Her eyes popped open in utter fear, and she realized her dicey predicament. The awkward kid was the serial killer, and her number was up. After slicing off her tongue, he slashed the knife back across the trachea and carotid. He turned on the shower and washed the blood off of himself, climbed out of the tub, and left her in the bathtub. He'd deal with the body in the morning.

Babe passed Estelle's place out of curiosity before leaving the Quarter. None of the lights were glowing on the second floor. Either people were getting busy, or the rooms hadn't filled for the hour yet. He wished Trey had let him go after the punk.

The doorman at the hospital greeted Babe, saying all company had left for the night, and his wife's progress was astonishing. The big guy could have done without the comment that when the doorman first saw her, there was no doubt she was a goner. The unit felt heavy with a hushed, stagnant quiet. Nurses moved quickly yet silently between the other patient's room and the desk. He knew that envelopment of quiet, the patient had died.

Lightly tapping on the sliding glass door, he slowly opened it. Trinity sat upright in the bed with her head cocked to the side. "Hey, you," she smiled. "There's a weird vibe around here. Do you have any idea what's going on?" He answered he had a good idea but wasn't sure. He asked if she knew the other patient. "I didn't know there was anyone else on this floor. I figured my dad, or you had something to do with that. Y'all are both so overprotective," and rolled her eyes.

Trinity was more than happy to regale her impressive progress in physical therapy. Babe smiled, one side of his lips sliding further back than the other. She grabbed his shirt and pulled him toward her. He kissed her. Out of the corner of his eye, he noticed her blanket move. "What do you have in bed with you?" He saw the movement again. She was bending her knee and straightening the leg out. She alternated between left and right. It was slow, but she was moving her legs unassisted. "Look at you. I told you, before long, you'll be dancing at Louie's." She eagerly told him she could move her legs, but they didn't hold her weight without support. "Do you realize how fast you are recovering? I've watched plenty of injured warriors struggling for six months, ten months, and longer. What you've done is a miracle, ma girl." She reminded him that her mom had been praying the Rosary like a wild woman. "Lady, God is hearing the constant stream of prayers and responding."

He curled his fists on top of each other, propping his chin. It was the closest he could get to her for quiet conversation. Babe updated her on the kid in the brown suit, asking if she remembered him telling her about the working girl Chop almost trafficked. No shocker, she did. "Hot pink wig?" He replied indeed, then proceeded to tell her how the kid tried to make her the next victim, but she got away, and one of the people from the market called the police. She had the detectives call him, and he went to the station. He'd been right; it was the acne-laden kid. "So, did you get him?"

"No, they told me I couldn't, and if I went against their reiterated order, I'd find myself on the wrong side of the cage." He repeated he wanted to get the motherfucker. Even though Gino had been his last vigilante maneuver, he was willing to make an exception to the twisted freak. His father, or sperm donor, Gino Vicarelli, was more of a personal vendetta rather than a vigilante act. All the others he'd accept that reference, but he looked at it like doing the world a favor. After an hour, she shooed him home. She pulled him down for another kiss and placed his hand on her breast. His breath caught in his throat. "Trinity, this won't get us anywhere. I want you desperately, but not until you come home and we have an okay from your doctors. My lady, you are still fragile."

Trinity squared her eyes, "You're gonna tell me you've been celibate, other than my cousin, and that whole debacle; it writhes under my skin. To think it was Bethany's idea blows me away. So how many times did you fuck her? Did you know it wasn't me each of those times?" Tears welled in her eyes. She was pissed. But more hurt than anything.

Babe held his head in his hands, "We gotta do this now?" She nodded as her bottom lip quivered. "I don't know, maybe three times. I desperately wanted you back, and even though things were different, I wanted to believe. The hard part was when I realized I didn't like this version of you. It tore me to pieces. When I found out for sure, I said some hurtful things to her, and I wish I hadn't, but I was angry. Fucking out of my head pissed. I felt betrayed by your mother, father, sister, everyone. The stupid fucking excuse was that I would keep the baby from them. I call bullshit on that." He could feel the heat rising on the back of his neck. Tears trickled down her cheeks. "I was a wreck, Trinity, and all I wanted was you back in my arms. The thing between us is an intense physical experience, and our souls link. I don't know your sexual history or what purpose it served for you, but sex to me was a basic need, not a co-mingling of spirit, that is, until you." Even though it sickened her stomach and she felt an ache of jealousy, she forgave him. She said her feelings toward her family were an entirely different anger, more like betrayal. "Trinity, they were hurting too. They'd lost your brother a few months before, and then to lose you was more than they could bear. They would fight to keep Chancée in their life—their only connection to you."

The heart-to-heart emotional flood ended up lasting another half hour. He kissed her good night.

Once the sun came up, Carlton woke and went into the bathroom for his morning piss. The lifeless, bloodied body wretched his stomach. It had nothing to do with the murder or the grotesque dead body, but he hadn't calculated how to dispose of the corpse. The bathroom window was nothing more than a vent, too small to shove a body through. Why hadn't he thought about the disposal of the body? He'd have to be more careful in the future. First and foremost in his mind was punishing the hooker who bloodied his nose. It would be complicated.

Carlton lay on the bed staring at the plain, dingy ceiling, wondering how many others had looked at the blank canvas and painted their own stories. Like a flipped light switch, it came to him. He remembered the hidden alcove where the blow job expert performed her mastery. He was sure she wasn't the only one to use the crafty hiding place. Carlton could pay someone on the street a hundred to lure her into the hidden play spot where he'd be waiting for her. There was one huge problem: the guy he paid to do the luring would know his face. He'd probably be in such shock when he quickly passed the blade along her throat that the guy's senses would react with hesitation, giving him enough time to plunge the knife deep into the sucker's gut, then he'd take back his money.

He jumped out of the bed and began practicing. Looking in the mirror, he enacted his plan. "Want to earn a fast hundred dollars." He hesitated as though giving the person a moment to react. He smiled at his reflection, "I see I have your attention." He raised his eyebrows with a smirk, "I have a special relationship with one of the prostitutes; I'll point her out to you once I locate her." He stepped back, "Man, you won't be wasting your time. After, I'll take you and Miss Hot Thing for food; no, that sounds too nerdy." He cleared his throat, "I'll buy you some food after. You." he pointed to the mirror with a flick pointing at his cocky too-cool stance, "Me and Miss Hot Thing. Starting to sound better?" Walking with a swagger, he turned sharply and waved the knife through the air as though slicing her throat, then abruptly turned and jabbed at the air three times. "Sorry, dude, you were a means to the end. Nothing personal." He coughed out a laugh, "Loser." He nodded at the mirror, raising his eyebrows and chin. He dressed in his jeans and tee shirt, but all he had were his suit shoes. He started smacking himself in the head. "I'm such a loser. I can't do anything right. I look like a freak with these stupid shoes." He sat on the floor and broke down sobbing.

There was a hard knock on his door. He'd paid in advance, so it wasn't the lady looking for money. A gruff male voice called through the door, "Kid, I saw you grab Shondra, and now she ain't answering her phone. She in there wit' you?" The man jiggled the door knob. "I know you in there, asshole. Where's she at?" He jammed his body into the door. At the rate he was going, he was causing such a ruckus that it would draw unwanted attention.

Carlton shouted, "Wait a minute, I'm on the crapper. I don't know where she went, swear."

He could hear the person on the other side of the door breathing hard. "I'm giving you two minutes to open the door, and then I'm coming in; it won't be pretty. I know she's in there; I heard you talking to her. Now open the fucking door."

Babe took his morning run with thoughts of Trinity racing through his mind. The sun was just rising, painting the sky with vibrant orange, pink, and even some purple. He wondered how much longer the doctors would keep her in the hospital. His mind flashed back to happier times, like when she wanted him to dance; Babe laughed out loud. She danced around him like he was a Maypole. Life had taken a lot of turns since his separation from the Corps. He'd ride out the storm if it meant the rest of his life would be with her. There was no doubt she was getting better by the day.

After a quick shower, he drove to the Quarter. There was a spot big enough for his truck outside Estelle's. It was a sign. Trinity had often said things were signs from God; he wasn't sure it was God's sign or something nefarious. He parked, entered, and started up the stairs. He heard a man yelling and banging on a door. *Fucking fools.* He made it up the stairs and listened to the man holler again, telling a boy to open the door that he knew someone was in there.

Babe stealthfully crept behind the man, who sprung like a cat when he felt the presence behind him. "You got a problem?" the big man asked.

The man began sputtering about some whore he'd paid the night before, and as she walked out of his room, the boy next door to him grabbed her. She willingly went into his room, but the man hadn't spoken to her since then. He figured she'd return to him because she'd left her feather boa. "Mister, look, I don't want no trouble, but I heard him talking to her, but, but, but he says she's not there. The boy's a liar." He spoke with peppered words and an exceedingly nervous tremble.

Babe moved the man to the side, leaned into the door, and shoved his shoulder against the door, which popped open like a Jack-in-the-box. It was the room of the acne-faced boy. Carlton stood holding a knife and swiping through the air, threatening both men. "Boy, don't pick a fight you can't win." The man spewed vomit when he saw the mutilated girl in the tub. Babe told the man to call nine-one-one and wait for the police downstairs. The man ran out the door and thundered down the steps. Babe heard as the front door closed. He lowered his head, looking at the kid with a glaring, sinister focus. "Time is up, Skippy. Give me the knife." The boy lunged toward the big man. In a flash, the Marine had the knife and carved a line up the insides of his wrists to the hinge in his elbow and dropped him to the floor. "Everyone will understand why you opened your veins after all the people that you've killed. Too bad you can only die once, motherfucker." He wiped the handle and placed it in each of the boy's hands, leaving only the whack-jobs prints, then laid the knife as though it had dropped out of his right hand. He saw as the life spilled out of the boy and grabbed a towel as though he were trying to save him. No one would be the wiser.

NOTHING BUT THE TRUTH

The street in front of Estelle's looked like staging from a crime drama. Blue lights strobed, the police blocked off the intersections, and looky-lous packed around the perimeter even though police tried to usher them away. To the working girls in the French Quarter, Estelle's had been a refuge from pimp-gone-wild times to clients with obsessions or delusions of rescuing the damsel in distress. It happened more than the average guy would think.

Trey and Max pulled up at the same time. Max talked to the client from the room next door to the killer. Estelle had been at the grocery store, but when she saw the crowd, she ran to the first cop to get the scoop and passage into the area. She hoped the serial killer hadn't murdered one of the girls who utilized her rooms on occasion.

The younger detective started up the staircase as Babe was heading out. "Fuck" he shook his head from side to side, biting his lip. "Babe, go back up. Didn't I tell you to leave the investigation to us? You get in more shit. What happened now?"

"I heard a commotion and reacted. The street door was open. Talk to the man who called y'all. I guess once the boy figured the man knew who he was, he offed himself. I tried to help stop the blood, but he opened both his wrists and bled out quickly; there was nothing I could do. By the way, he's got a corpse in his room, warning; it even turned my stomach. I hope you didn't just eat. I'm on my way to see Trinity. Call if you need me." Babe turned as though he was heading down the stairs.

Trey grabbed the big guy's arm, "I'm afraid not. You had to get involved. Marine, you are now part of this crime scene—like it or not. Stay. Do.Not.Move." The detective was pissed and wasn't taking shit from anyone. It had been a rough several days. Trey called Max. "Better come up. You're not gonna believe this shit." He proceeded down the hall to the open door at the end. It was evident what had happened. The dead guy was exactly as described to the sketch artist. He was just a screwed-up kid, but still a kid with a life in front of him, now gone.

Max made it to the top of the stairs and grunted, "I'm getting too old for this shit." Looking up, he saw the Hulk standing to the side with his hands clasped behind his back. "Heya, Babe. It looks like Captain Treyhole punished you to the corner. What happened here?" Trey hollered to Max to move it.

"Warning, Sledge, the scene is gruesome, head's up." The big man pointed down the hall to an opened door.

Babe heard strings of cursing coming from the end of the hall. He heard them say the Crime Lab and the Coroner were en route. Since there was nothing he could do, he texted Trinity.

Babe: Good Morning, Sleeping Beauty.

Trinity: GM to you, Prince Charming. LOL

Babe: Got the guy. Holding me for questioning.

Trinity: How long ya think they'll keep you?

Babe: Trey is pissed I was here.

Trinity: I hope he won't keep you too long. I love you

Babe: Me too. Right back atcha.

A racket ensued outside the building. Babe figured the Crime Lab was trying to get as close as possible. He knew his truck was parked in the worst possible place for them to navigate toward the entrance.

After about ten minutes, he heard the rattling of the gurney and loud thuds as it hit treads coming up the stairs. The woman leading the way checked Babe out as she passed. He wondered if she would think he was the villain, but her expression didn't reflect a negative vibe. The man at the rear recognized the big guy calling him by name. Babe nodded, commenting, "You'll need a second body bag. It's a bloody mess in there."

Babe was frustrated; the ordeal took up too much of his day. He should have gotten out of there quicker. He called Mays, who picked up after two rings, "Hey, little brother. How are you, and how is Trinity?" He leaned against the wall, wishing he could bug out.

"Good to hear your voice, Mays. It's been a hot mess down here, as I'm sure you've seen on the tube, but it's over. The killer committed suicide; I was on the scene. He was a strange kid, probably eighteen at the most. Sad, really. Trinity has suddenly started recovering at lightning speed. She's talking and taking steps with assistance. And you? How are the kids?"

Mays laughed, "So, let me get this right. You were on the scene when the boy took his life. Are you sure you didn't help it along?"

"Fuck, no. I tried to help."

"My ass, Babe. Tell your story to someone else." Babe cleared his throat. "Just yankin' your chain, bro." Mays sighed loudly. "Everyone is good here. I still haven't heard a peep from Lissa. Talk about strange. You grow a baby in your belly for nine months and then disappear and exit their lives like it's no big deal. It's weird; they don't appear to miss her either. So fucking bizarre. It's just the opposite with my mom and dad. Mom stops in constantly to check on the kids and me. They are freaked and don't understand, but it is what it is, ya know? I'm glad to hear your lady is doing better. That is an answer to many prayers. Where are you right now?"

Babe went into the scenario explaining Trey, the detective, made him stay where the murder-suicide took place. They talked for the next half hour, with Mays doing most of the talking. He told Babe his practice was booming even though he'd cut back hours to be with the kids.

Max came from the room; Babe quickly ended the call with Mays.

"Marine, you done pissed Trey off like I haven't seen in a while. Even though you heard a disturbance, you shoulda kept on going. He plans on hauling your ass to the precinct for questioning. He says your coincidental appearances are getting on his nerves. I think he plans to punish you for ignoring his command. Look, I know all you want to do is help, but sometimes, it makes the situation worse. Our new boss has a hard-on for playing by the rules and is gonna lean on Trey and me hard for an explanation as to why you were here. Just sayin'." Max sucked his teeth and clicked with a sigh. "Don't make no plans for the day is all I'm sayin'."

Trey came through the doorway. He was on the phone, and from his expression, he was being bitched out. The young detective squinted his eyes, shaking his head with a fuming look. He briskly gestured to Babe to follow him. His responses were respectful, with an edge of impatience as he spoke to Big Jim, his new supervisor. "Yes, sir. No problem, sir. I got it. He's someone you want to meet. The Marine has helped us with a few cases. No, sir, it is not his job, but he brings a lot to the table." Trey rolled his eyes at Babe and ended the call. "What the fuck, Vicarelli? My boss is up my ass sideways. He does not want you to come to the station, saying he has no time for making you a catch 'em hero celebrity. Ya see you're taking the spotlight from him. Not cool, asshole. Get the fuck out of here, and for crying out loud, I don't care if you see someone getting ready to kill someone; keep on going and just call us. Am I clear?"

"Crystal."

Babe wasted no time and got out of there.

Babe told Siri to call Trinity. "Hey, good lookin', I'm on my way to you. I should be there in ten minutes. Can I pick something up for you?" She said no, that all she needed was him.

He passed a florist and, with a reflex action, pulled over, hopped out, and purchased a dozen roses. Pulling out onto St. Charles Avenue, his phone buzzed. "Vicarelli."

"Captain, it's Collins. Are you still contemplating returning to service?" Babe started to say something, but Collins continued, "Sir, I've been giving it some thought, and since I hadn't heard back from you, I figured you decided against it, but what about Reserves? Just a thought."

Babe said he thought it was a good idea and would get back to him. He relayed the change in his situation and briefly brushed over the issue with Trinity. Daniel quieted then, with a shaky voice, responded with condolences. Babe reassured him the future was looking brighter and that he was on his way to be with his wife, complete with a fistful of roses. *Something more to look into. Always something.* After a few back-and-forth questions, they ended the call. The Reserve was food for thought. It would equate to one weekend a month, including the application, physical exam, psych evaluation, and other assorted hoops, such as rigorous training, which he looked forward to. One thing was for sure: the Marines put an applicant through the mill. They had no room for slouchers. Time was moving quickly, and he needed to make his mind up fast.

He spoke into the phone, "Call Coach."

"Hello Vicarelli. How's it going?" He sounded upbeat, and Babe could hear a woman's voice in the background.

Watching the traffic as it came to a slow roll with the flash of brake lights as people ran up each other's ass. "Did you ever consider re-upping, sir? I'm thinking about the Reserves. Civilian life doesn't suit my personality, but I have a wife and a family. Full-time service wouldn't be ideal. I'm not saying I haven't thought about it."

"Why not go Fed, like FBI, ATF, DEA? I have connections with all of the above. Most of the time, it'll be a nine to fiver. I don't know if that's up your bailiwick." Coach crunched something into the phone. Babe asked if it was an inconvenient time to talk. "Ice, I've gotten into the habit of chewing ice. My dentist has a fit. Besides being driven crazy by civilians, how are things? Trinty? The baby?"

"Much to tell, sir." He briefly, as he had with Daniel, told the Trinity story.

"Son, if there's anything I or my wife can do, let us know." With a sigh, the Coach hesitated but asked, "What happened to the person who inflicted the injuries?"

Babe pulled alongside the hospital and parked. "Eliminated, but not by my hand. It's a convoluted story, and one day, maybe over a whiskey, I'll tell you the gruesome series of events."

"Copy that. Take care, son." Their conversation ended.

Babe carried the bouquet of roses up to her room.

Trinity was the image of perfection. She had brushed her hair and braided it down the side, added a touch of makeup, and wore her favorite Saints loungewear. "Look at my girl, all dolled up for visitors."

"For you." She batted her eyes. "I have news," she said with a flirty laugh. "If I keep progressing as I am, the doc said I might be discharged in a couple of weeks and have PT at home." She looked down, biting the side of her bottom lip. "I kinda lied. I said we had all the equipment I'd need at the house. The doctor seemed surprised and questioned about those supports I walk through, you know, the bars."

He laughed at the 'kinda lied'; there was no kinda involved. Trinity knew how to manipulate her way into getting what she wanted. The thought crossed his mind that the sprucing up may have had to do with her working the doc. She looked hot, no doubt about it. She was nothing but skin and bones, but she didn't seem as gaunt in her clothes and tidied appearance. "Oh, the biggest news, you can get in bed with me if you can fit. He said you probably couldn't, but I have an idea. How about you stretch out on the bed and pull me on top of you? It might take some negotiating my legs." She was sitting in bed with her legs crossed under her. She straightened one leg, helping the leg with her arms, but she had most definitely used the muscles in her leg and glutes. She mimicked the motion with her other leg.

He grinned, took off his boots, then leaned over and picked her up, carrying her like a baby with his arms under her. He sat on the bed, and with his right hand on her thighs, he helped her straighten her body on top of his. Laying back, he chuckled, "And now what?" She kissed him with intensity. "No point in starting something we can't finish."

Trinity squinted her eyes and pouted like a child, "Who says we can't? I don't remember anyone telling me I couldn't." She ground her hips on him. It didn't take much to awaken the heat.

"Trinity Marie!" her mother's voice echoed through the room. Babe looked Trinity eye to eye as she burst into laughter. The big guy felt his face flush with embarrassment. He imagined it was what the boys felt when he'd bust them making out with a girl. She rolled off the top of him against one of the bedside rails. As he moved out of the bed, he started to apologize to her mother. "Babe, you don't have to tell me; I know whose big idea this was. She has you wrapped around her little finger." He quickly sat and secured his boots, letting the heat cool.

Before he could say another word, his phone buzzed. It was a call from Trey. "Vicarelli," he answered.

Trey told him to come to the station. Captain James, "Big Jim" Campbell requested his presence. *Oh, fuck.*

He leaned over and kissed Trinity, "Trey wants me to come to the station." He turned to her mom, "Sorry, our meeting was odd, and I have to meet Detective Kimble."

Antoinette appeared concerned. "Do you need me to call our attorney?"

"No, ma'am, I am an attorney," he smiled. Those who knew him often forgot he was a man of many skills and education.

Everyone in the squad room seemed to be writing reports. The city had been a swarming hive of crime, which wasn't counting City Slasher. Finally, they could put that one to rest. Swirling in Trey's mind were questions regarding the Marine being there on happenstance. Granted, Babe had told him he knew where the guy lived and had seen him. Trey imagined Babe had been one hell of a Marine and a force to reckon with. It was impressive that he'd gotten involved in hunting sex traffickers, and his instincts were undeniable. There was no doubt in Trey's mind that he was a good guy, but in his gut was a smidge of unsettled feelings of uncertainty.

"Let me know as soon as your friend the Marine arrives," the captain barked. The new boss was transparent; he held contempt for anyone who outshone him. As he referred to himself and encouraged others to call him, Big Jim was nearly six-three with a girth of around thirty-eight. He wasn't jelly fat but had more jiggle than he cared to admit. Because Babe was a massive man, he had a hard time calling anyone big, tiny, fat, skinny; in his opinion, there was no need for the description in a name. People knew what they were; he was confident in his musculature but worked daily to maintain it. Granted, his body was prone to muscle buildup, as he suspected his nephew was one of Mays' sons. Given that Mays hadn't worked out or tried for fitness, he leaned more toward the body of someone who enjoyed rich foods and drinks. Since their first encounter, he had quickly changed his shape and created contours similar to Babe's.

Trey met the big guy when he walked through the entrance. "Warning: the boss is an egomaniac and takes himself way too seriously. By the way, you and I still need to talk. I need to get right with myself, but we can do it later." Trey led Babe toward the captain's office. The man stood at the entrance to his office with a puffed-out chest and a stance that screamed superiority.

Babe put out his hand, "I've heard about you, Captain Campbell. I'm Babe Vicarelli. What can I do for you, sir?"

Big Jim waved him into the office and took note of the man's massive size. Babe waited for the bossman to take a seat before sitting. "Sit. I've heard an assortment of stories about you and how you've helped the department before. Things will be different in my department; unlike my predecessor, I frown upon any Tom, Dick, or Harry getting into the fray. Someone could always get injured, and then the city would be responsible, and my head would be on a platter. Am I clear?"

"Crystal clear, sir. I understand proper protocol and chain of command." He noticed the older man glance at the tattoo on his deltoid. Only part was exposed. The man pointed at Babe's tattoo and asked if he had served. "Yes, sir. I served in special ops for the Corps. I am a Raider, sir."

"Thank you for your service, Marine," Babe responded by thanking him for his, commenting the streets of New Orleans could be as hostile as many wartorn places in the world. "If you see something, call us; do not, I repeat, do not take things into your own hands. Understood?" Babe nodded but wanted to say if someone fucked with him or his family, then they'd get what was coming to them, like it or not. Re-upping was sounding more and more palatable. Civilian life was not for him. Big Jim reviewed what Trey had said about Babe and the City Slasher. "Now, what you told Detective Kimble is the whole truth? You didn't leave anything out?" Babe told him it was nothing but the truth.

After another fifteen minutes of hearing how great of a job the captain did with a police department in Memphis. He planned to turn New Orleans around. *Good luck; you might want to get your head out of your ass first.* The Captain closed out their meeting; at least it was better than the Noelle way, no good-bye, hasta la vista, fuck you, just a sharp dismissal.

CHESTNUT BOUND

The manner in which the new Captain spoke was indeed the words of someone who fancied himself like the second coming. He carried on with an air of superiority, speaking down condescendingly, which irked Babe. When commanding those in his unit, he fought alongside them, hustled more, and was the one to put himself out front. Trey had been correct; the guy was an egomaniac and all but required genuflection—*Pompass ass.*

Trey snagged him before Babe made it to the door. He brought the big man into the squad's break room; it was empty. Eye to eye, the detective was sincere in his questions. "What's the deal? How is it that you know things like where the slasher lived? You seem to be one step ahead of us and in step with the perpetrators. What's the formula you use? If anything, you are consistent."

He silently sat for the first few moments, perhaps trying to formulate an answer to the string of questions. "Detective, I have no formula, so to speak. What can I say? I've always managed life in a state of alertness and aware of my surroundings. I guess because of my rough upbringing, I lived on the edge, wondering when the next punch or slap would strike me. Needless to say, it keeps one on their toes. Since I can remember, I've been a quiet person, conjuring possible outcomes of everyday actions and sizing up people. I have a knack for it, if I'm not distracted, a la Trinity. When I start feeling a tingling sensation, I know something is about to go down—so I rely on my senses by listening and observing, not talking. That's my best guess." He placed his hands on his thighs and sat still, giving Trey a moment to absorb his comment. He very well couldn't say he knew how the deranged thought because he was a monster. "Listen, watch, and turn on your, as my boys call it, spidey senses."

Even though there was a price Trey had to pay: the tyranny of his overzealous superior, he thanked Babe for hunting down the City Slasher. No sooner did their conversation end when Babe was back en route to Chestnut.

The music on the radio was upbeat and made him think of Trinity. Hell, everything made him visualize Trinity, filling his stomach with tickles bubbling up to his throat and sending shock waves below the belt. He pulled into the driveway, noticing a white truck parked across the street. Gunner was in the backyard and all over Babe when he entered the yard. The dog was edgier than usual and had pacing energy.

When Babe opened the door, Gunner bee-lined and stood at the coat closet door, barking, growling, and scratching. *Odd*. Other than the dog, the rest of the house was eerily silent. He pulled out his knife, ready for battle, but running through his head was *never bring a knife to a gunfight*. He silently moved to the laundry room and grabbed his hidden Sig from the top cabinet. No one could reach it but him. He checked for ammunition and loaded her up. The big man returned to the coat closet, where Gunn was still clamoring to open the door. He had marred the door, door frame, and wall next to the closet with deep grooves from his claws.

Babe stood silently to the side of the door; Gunn started to calm, and then, with a sudden burst, he opened the closet quickly and forcefully. A long-whiskered man about five-nine fired two wild shots before the big man, and Gunn pinned him to the floor. The Marine held the muzzle to the base of his skull. "You picked the wrong house, motherfucker." He kicked the man's weapon aside, pulled him up by the scruff of his neck, and threw him into a hard-backed chair with a powerful slug to the jaw. Babe snapped his fingers at the stunned man. Gunner stood guard in front of the intruder, baring a most frightening snarl. Babe called upstairs, "Ruthie, Chris, Reg, Jacob, everything is safe." Above his head, he could hear the rumbling of footsteps by the boys, and then Ruthie slowly came down the stairs with Chancée. "Good job, ma'am."

She walked up to the seated bedraggled man and slapped him across the face. "Who you think you is comin' up in our house? Mister, you got a lot of nerve." It was at that point Babe noticed blood dripping from the man's pant leg and decisive tears in his pants around the calf.

Babe towered over him. "Give me your I.D. and pull your left pant leg up." He glanced at the picture I.D. In the photo, his hair was just below his ear lobes, and the beard was cropped short. "Willis P. Spindell, before I call the authorities, I want to know why you felt you could waltz into my house and scare my caretaker and children?"

The stranger looked at the floor and said he'd seen the boys playing in the yard and that Jacob looked like his son, although he hadn't seen him since he was three. The street girls his mother worked with kicked him out and wouldn't let him visit the boy. Once she died, the girls made sure he would never see the boy again. All he wanted was to talk to the boy. Babe asked why the gun. The man said he'd knocked on the door once but got scared and left, then he got his courage up, and when the boys ran inside from playing ball, he took the liberty to let himself in; that's when the dog went after him. His eyes darted around the room the whole time, refusing to look at the massive man.

"Jacob, come here. Do you recognize this man?" The boy looked hard at the man, but Babe could tell nothing registered.

"No, sir. I've never seen him before. Maybe I look like his son, but he's not my father. The john that fathered me, from what the girls told me, was Hispanic. There was a kid two years younger than me, and everyone thought we were brothers, but we weren't. Mister, maybe that's your kid, but this is now my dad," and he put his arm around Babe's waist.

THE IMPOSTOR LIE

Babe mentioned he still hadn't answered the question about the gun. He said it was in case he had a gun. An eyebrow raised, "So, you knew this was my house and still had the audacity to enter uninvited?" He glanced at the boys, "You three can go outside or upstairs, but I'm going to have a conversation with Willis Spindell, adults only. Ruthie, if you would take our princess outside or in the nursery, I wouldn't want to offend either of you."

The big guy waited until they left. He grabbed the man's face. "Willis, my inclination is to kill you on the spot, but I'm trying to change my ways, so I'm going to let the law handle you, but fair warning, you stupid motherfucker, come anywhere near my house again, and I will kill you, and that's a promise. Are we clear?"

The man answered, "Crystal."

"Crystal? You sure don't come across as military. What branch?"

He looked down, "I was Navy." The next question Babe asked concerned his discharge—honorably or dishonorably. How many tours, how many years in, and all the usual questions? Babe called Coach Kennedy, his go-to for advice.

"Vicarelli, how's your wife? I've been thinking about you lately. You've made great strides, son, almost a conversationalist." He let out a gravelly chuckle. "Had to pull your leg, Vic. Now, is this a social call, or can I help you?" Like always, the man was point-blank; there was no need to beat around the bush. Coach had always been a straight shooter with him.

Babe sat in a chair adjacent to the intruder, keeping a watchful eye on him. He went through the accounts of the interlude.

"You've grown, son. The old you would have shot first and asked questions later. Your demons are falling to the wayside; if not, they've entirely left the building," he chuckled. "I know you still have one or two connections in the Corps. Maybe they might know. I'm proud of you for using your noggin instead of those fists. Your intruder must be a few cans short of a six-pack. I am at a loss for advice other than to touch base with an active blast from the past." The conversation ended, and he was still no wiser. Decisions about handling the guy were up in the air.

Daniel was the first person to come to mind, but he was tired of talking and communicating with anyone but Trinity and his family—and sometimes even that was a bit overwhelming. Maybe he should drop him at the VA and call it a day. Something was under his skin, and it all didn't add up. "Where do you live?"

"In Kenner."

"Then, how the fuck did you happen by my yard and see the boys playing? You're a long way from Kenner, pal." The man blinked hard as though trying to focus. Babe had caught him in a lie. Then it twigged; somebody had sent him, but the knowledge of his home on Chestnut was still unknown, except for Javier, his brother, and a handful of the kids' friends. "You fucking liar. Who sent you here?"

"No one, I swear." His voice tremored. "No one." Babe walked to the back of the chair and leaned in, calling bullshit on his answer. He grabbed the man and dragged him into the garage. Babe tied and hoisted him to the support eye holding his heavyweight bag. He stretched the man's arms overhead, taped his mouth closed with silver electrical tape, and put on his workout gloves. The man tried to yell to no avail. His eyes pleaded for forgiveness. *Not this time, pal,* Babe thought. He knew his fists would have caused more pain, but there was no point in scuffing up his hands. Maybe after a few days of beatings, the loser's lips might start confessing.

Round one began as Babe jabbed toward the jaw; the gut punches fired one after the other. The man didn't take long to pass out between the jabs and punches. The big guy removed his gloves and headed into the kitchen. Chris was in the kitchen, and Ruthie held the baby. "Thank Gawd, you came home when you did, sir. Did the police take him away?" She tested the temperature of Chancée's bottle on her wrist. Babe didn't answer.

After watching Chris, he noticed the boy was becoming more of a man; his body was filling out, and it was apparent he'd been lifting. "Chris, make sure you tell the others that the garage is off-limits until further notice." Ruthie's head spun toward him with squared-off eyes and a face exuding displeasure. Babe took his cup of ice and water into the garage and locked the door.

He doused the man in the face, waking him to consciousness. Babe ripped the tape from his mouth. "Look, I'll tell you whatever you want to know." The man pleaded.

"How'd you know where I live? Who sent you to find me?" Babe grilled.

"I followed you from work." The man lied.

"Oh, and just where do I work?" He asked.

"Uh-um." The man began to try to stall, his eyes jumping from one side of the garage to the other. Perspiration formed tiny beads above his lips. Most of his face had started to bloom with red, purple, and pink patches, eventually turning to hideous bruises. Swelling was another problem, but most of all, it was the undeniable fear painted on the man's face. It was with just cause. The man delivering punishment was monstrous and had strength, unlike anything he'd felt before.

"Exactly, you piece of shit." He re-taped his mouth, and the punishment resumed. Body blows, chin jabs, then a purposeful cross to his face, and the man's lights went out. Babe sat on the hood of the car with his back toward the door and the unconscious bound man in front of him. "You stupid bastard. I want the truth." There was a light knock on the door. It was Jacob asking him to open the door. "I'll be out in a minute, Jake." The man's demeanor and ways felt familiar, but he couldn't place it. He wasn't a thug like Antoine's men, but he wasn't Hispanic like Javier's crew. This was different. One way or the other, he was a lying, weasely piece of shit. *Ah, Chop!* This cunt had ties to the man Babe swore to kill a couple of years before and caused his life a living hell. He had gotten sidetracked with other strange circumstances. Civilian life for Babe was never a dull moment.

Chris, Reg, Jacob, and Ruthie waited when he walked out to get the hose. Sweat rolled down his flushed face. Ruthie began the interrogation. "What you doin' in there?" Babe brought the hose under the door.

"Working on the heavyweight." It wasn't a lie, maybe an omission of fact.

"Then, why can't the boys work out with you?" She quizzed.

He slightly tilted his head, "Because I want some alone time. Thank you." The sarcasm was thick.

She pointed to the house. "Boys, go inside, and I'll be there momentarily." She waited until they were out of earshot. "Do you have that man in the garage?"

Babe looked upward, then back down to her. "Do you really want to know?"

She stood stiffly, "Yes, sir, I do." The determination on her face was palpable.

"I do, and he will remain there until I get honest answers. Anything else you want to know?"

Ruthie cast her eyes downward, "I suppose not; I guess you know what you're doing, but there will be no taking of life on your grandfather's property, which includes the garage." She raised an eyebrow as she pursed her lips.

Babe gave his word that there'd be no killing on the property. Tumbling thoughts ricocheted in his mind. The intruder's personality and demeanor were a match to Chop's. Maybe someone followed Javier and was looking for the kingpin; after all, he had said there were attempts on his life.

He dragged the hose into the garage. The next question would pertain to Tim Faraday. Babe pinched the hose to stop any water flow, attached a nozzle, and gave it a test squeeze. *Perfect.* He doused him with the remaining ice water. With eyes at half mast and one swelling almost to closure, he moaned, "Fuck you, Babe." The military man smiled, thinking, *ah, now we're getting somewhere.*

He sprayed him in the face. "Who are you, Willis Spindell, and what do you want with me? Once again, who sent you?" Babe sat with a scowl, eyebrows furrowed, and a look of the Grim Reaper in his expression.

"Okay, okay, okay. I'll give you what you want."

Three weeks before going to New Orleans, Willis and five of his buddies were playing cards for money. They started with the braggadocious bullshit. This one beat up three dudes, another knifed a guy who looked like a WWE wrestler, and then the man who usually sat back and listened decided to speak.

He was a scrawny guy with a has-been appearance. His hair was long and scraggly to go with his unkempt beard. The crevices carved in his face were from too many drugs and hard living. He pushed up the sleeve of his tee shirt and spoke with a puffed-up chest of machismo. "Y'all see this scar? The toughest motherfucker I've ever known carved my Marine tattoo off my arm, but before he done that, I kicked his ass, threw him in the back of my car, and brought him to my boss. For some reason, my boss took a shine to the massive Marine, Captain Babe Vicarelli. Before I knew it, they were tight like this." He held up crossed fingers. "I'm still looking to get revenge on him. He killed my brother." Dumb as dirt, Willis continued in the card game despite his mounting debt. When all was said and done, Willis owed the helo pilot five hundred dollars with no way of paying.

Chop demanded his money. Willis answered with a high-pitched, squeaky voice of fear. "Look, I'll get it, but it'll take a few days."

"You came to this game with two hundred fifty dollars and now owe me five big ones since doubling down." He pulled out a wrinkled and worn picture of Babe. "This man hangs by a place in New Orleans called Louie's Tap; follow him for a few days. He's disappeared, but I know he's around. I'll consider your debt paid if you can gather intel on him. Like where he works, lives, and if he is still seeing his hot little piece of ass. You don't gotta do nothin'; just get me the information.

Willis continued with his story. "I found you at the bar, but it took me a few days to see where you went; you're hard to follow." The beaten man went on to say that he thought he saw him pull up to the house, but a lady answered the door, and there were a bunch of kids making noise, so he figured it was the wrong house. "I called Tim and told him I'd keep looking. I didn't know where you worked at; I hadn't figured that one out and that you didn't have no old lady, but I was close to finding your digs. I saw your car pull into the garage; I was waiting a block away. That's no bullshit."

Babe read him as he spoke despite the split, swollen lips. He'd fiercely beat him. The story seemed plausible; the decision to follow was more complicated. Did he find Chop and put that portion of his life to rest once and for all, or did he let the guy give Chop all the info and lay in wait for him? The answer: It'd be better if he were nowhere near New Orleans. He left the man tied in the garage and pulled his truck up close. He swung in at an angle so the passenger door was more convenient and closest to the garage door. He went back in and clocked the man in the jaw, rendering him unconscious. Babe quickly put the dead weight in the back seat and drove to one of the housing projects, where he dropped the body after torquing his neck. A white junkie degenerate in the neighborhood would be toast and give the appearance of a drug deal gone bad. The police rarely did deep investigations into the projects unless they involved a child.

Babe texted Ruthie: Gone for a couple of days. And I abided by your request - no dead bodies. LOL.

If someone were to read the text, they would think it was a private joke.

He removed the man's cell from his pocket, looked at his recent calls, and recognized Chop's phone number. He texted:

Babe: Found his crib. No girl. Work? On way to you

Chop: Stay N.O. McDonald's on Canal tomorrow at 3

Babe: Where to stay

Chop: in car

With the connection made, he wanted to let Trinity know he might be busy for a day or two, not to worry, and to get Javier's blessing on Chop. He called Trinity, and she picked up the phone right away.

"Where you at, Babe?"

"On my way to you, hot thing." She seemed overly happy and had something to show him. "Will it be appropriate?" He responded with a single laugh.

"Boy, totally. Love you to the moon and back." The call ended.

Babe pondered what she wanted to show him. He hoped she wasn't looking for a booty call, not that he didn't desire her, but not until the doctor gave the okay. She was still so frail. While her personality was back to Miss Sassy Pants, her body was weak.

It was time to text Javier.

Babe: How's it hangin'?

Javier: Always a little to the left. What's up, big man?

Babe: Your helo guy is causing me problems again. I'm gonna end this part of the story.

Javier: Sounds like a plan

Babe: Copy that.

Now, he had a permission slip to execute. It would feel good and be closure to that chapter of his life.

Babe strolled into the hospital like he owned the place. Finally, setting the stage to eliminate Chop lightened his load and maybe closed the book on war stories. There was an element of sadness, perhaps disappointment. Tim "Chop" Faraday wasn't the courageous steel-balled helo pilot he championed. Maybe it was better to have a clear picture of the sort of scum he was, but it had all the earmarks of betrayal that left a sour taste in his mouth.

Would he find pleasure in eliminating Chop, or would it weigh heavy on his newly found soul? He tracked back to the night the pilot showed up at Louie's. Had he known then what he knew now, he would have carried his ass to a darkened alley and put a stop to the piece of shit. It was funny as he thought about how one change in the journey affected the entire story. He would have never met Javier, learned of The Commander's turncoat, or found out about the abduction of children for the sole purpose of sexual perversion. Chris, Reg, and Jacob wouldn't be a part of his life. That thought felt like a dull blade penetrating his gut. It dawned on him that he loved those boys. Those were the lessons the God entity wanted him to learn. *Hey God, lesson learned.*

Now for Trinity's surprise. Part of him pictured her naked in bed, but he quickly pushed the image from his mind. Trepidatiously, he slid the door open. "Big man, I've left my surprise for you. It's a show, not a tell. She sat straight in the bed, leaned to her left, pulled the wheelchair over, and it opened with a determined flick of her wrist; then, she held on with both hands and moved her body into the chair. She had to adjust her legs on the footrests, but he could see a slight muscle development in her legs. "What choo think about that?" Her face was beaming with a pale crimson beneath her caramel skin. "Not only can I get myself in and out of bed, but I can transfer to a regular chair and get myself down to therapy."

Babe's smile shone brightly, "Impressive, my girl. Are we going down to therapy right now?" She smiled and nodded. She rolled out of the room to the elevator, pressed the button, exited, punched the code in, and rolled in as the door opened. She managed everything by herself. She put the braces on with ease and lifted herself to a standing position between the bars.

Her P.T. guy jogged over. "No, ma'am. I see you trying to show off, but you know the belt goes on before you stand. Watch your lady walk the bars." It was a concentrated one foot at a time, but no rest between steps. She almost walked normally. "Sir, as you can see, her gait is near perfect; we just gotta strengthen the legs and teach them how to support her body." He pointed at Trinity, "This is one determined lady." The therapist watched her closely, especially in the turn, ready to step in. Babe said he had a leg press at home and just about anything one could want in a gym. He admitted he'd have to install parallel bars but would do so immediately. "Give her a few more days, then I don't see why she can't go home. She can have P.T. come to the house. Babe had to make a few adjustments, such as a lift chair for the stairs. They'd keep a wheelchair at the ready both upstairs and downstairs. "Sir, this is all conjecture on my part. Her doctor has the final say. I'll talk with him in favor of a release."

Trinity chirped in, "Please tell him to release me so I can have sex." Babe put his hand over his eyes and shook his head. "Really, and like are there better positions given my condition."

The therapist started to laugh and agreed that he would ask the doctor. He looked at Babe who shrugged and said it was all her. After lifting weights and a few more upper body and leg exercises, they returned to her room.

Trinity transferred into the bed flawlessly. "You were right, big surprise. I'll get to work on getting the house ready for you. The boys and Ruthie will come tomorrow if you don't mind. Before you ask, yes, they will bring Chancée.

The entire way home, thoughts consumed his mind. First thing in the morning, he had to call a medical supply place and arrange for all the new equipment, but then he had to abduct Chop. Where to take him? There would be workers in the garage at his house; he couldn't drag him through the hotel. *Think, think, think.* He could see a For Sale sign in his mind, but where was it? He veered off and headed to River Road. It was dark, but the sign was large if his memory served him right. Sure enough, the sign he remembered was on a small, dilapidated warehouse. A chain link fence surrounded the perimeter, and a small lock was the only thing holding the gate closed. *No problem.* Then, he thought about the meat puzzle Carlton, the City Slasher, attempted to create. There were dumpsters everywhere. He remembered seeing an old rusty chainsaw in the garage at home. It would be perfect for the dismemberment. Payback was going to be a motherfucker.

Everything was quiet when he entered. He silently moved through the house and up the stairs. Having her home would be an answer to a prayer. *Okay, I'm trying to get with the program.* He peeked in on Chancée, who was fast asleep.

Staring up at the ceiling, he put the details into a precise plan. The first thing he'd do was break the chain on the gate, hoping no one noticed. Then, hot-wire Willis' white truck and wait in the parking lot of the McDonalds on Canal. He'd jam a couple of crumpled fast food bags on the dashboard for authenticity. He had the guy's sunglasses and baseball cap, which didn't fit. He'd grab one of his own. Willis had a gray hoodie and jeans. *Yep*, he thought, he could pull that off. Slouching in the seat would make him appear smaller. With a dropped head, he'd appear resting, but after Chop pulled in, the crème de la crème was a text that told him to follow; he'd found where Babe worked. The ride to the warehouse would end with the brutal death of Tim Faraday. He played with the bull, and now he would get the horns in a big way.

HEADS OR TAILS

*W*hile in his mind, it seemingly all came together, but then there was reality. Babe sat biding his time in the McDonald's parking lot. Chop was running late; what a surprise. At three thirty-six, he pulled up in an old Cadillac Seville. It would have been a vehicle Gino Vicarelli would have drooled over back in the day. *No good piece of excrement*, he thought. The choice of wheels was no surprise; Chop always thought too highly of himself. Babe texted from Willis' phone.

Babe: Follow me.

Chop: Hold your horses. I'm running in for a burger and fries.

Babe checked him out in the rearview mirror. The man looked even worse for wear than he had a couple of years back during bullshit abduction time. What a cluster that had been. Since then, he'd had several reminders to sharpen his acute skills of tuning into strange behavior and dangerous scum. Babe was flawlessly tuned into the mission at hand. He parked the truck at the exit's side, making it easy for Chop to follow. Bag in one hand and burger in the other, Chop crossed to his car and slipped inside exactly as Babe had hoped. He pulled in right behind the white truck.

When they turned from Carrollton onto River Road, Chop called. Babe acted like he didn't hear and turned the radio loud. Then, a ding came through.

Chop: Where the fuck we going?

Babe: A warehouse.

Chop: What's he do there?

Babe: How the fuck do I know? I didn't stop and ask questions.

The white truck pulled inside the gate and off to the side. Chop drove straight ahead. *Perfect.* There was a host of machinery, but no one was working. He saw the scrapwood makeshift office and crept to the door. Gun in hand, ready to shoot, he flung the door open. It was an empty office. Perplexed, he left the office. Babe followed close, reached out, overpowered him with one hand, and squeezed his arm with the gun, which dropped on the concrete.

"Yo, Vic, you scared the shit out of me." Chop tried to pull from Babe's grasp. Unsuccessful. "Why you holdin' me so hard?" Silence from the big guy.

He shoved Chop into a chair. "Don't move. You've been coming into my shit, messing with my family, and it's over. Javier gave me his blessing. Now you have a choice. My original plans were to sever you at every joint, inflicting the most pain I could until you passed out from blood loss, but since I once thought of you as a stand-up guy, I thought I'd let you choose. Slice across the throat, break your neck, or fight me, and then I dismember you—first your fingers and toes, then hands and feet, and so on. You get the picture. You'll be one fuckin' meat puzzle." The helo pilot vomited.

Chop begged for mercy. He promised he'd go away and never appear again.

"We tried that motherfucker, and you lied. I've given you choices, so what is it? You wanna fight me? You're a wiry bastard; who knows, maybe you will escape from my grip, maybe not, but you know the consequence of a fight." Babe flipped his hand up and down, like either or. "The thing I don't get is, why did you want me dead long before I killed your brother?" Chop couldn't answer; he had no idea. It just popped into his head because he wanted Trinity. And Babe was just collateral damage. The big guy nodded. There sounded some truth in what he said, but it still went back to the original question about which death he'd prefer—any which way it was going to happen.

Chop stared at Babe. "Captain, did it ever occur to you that everyone in the unit, hell, anyone you came in contact with, looked at you like a demi-god? You know how they looked at me? I was the crazy helo jockey who would go where no one else would go—that's the glory I got. My wife was fucked up before I got home, and once I was home, it was a fuckin nightmare. Did you know I had to decide between eventual incarceration, according to my dad, or the military? It was hell for most of us, but it all came naturally for you. You were the one with the balls of steel."

Babe had enough of the pity party and called it quits, asking once again what method of death he chose. Chop stood, took off his outer shirt, and raised his fists. He started dancing with fancy footwork, such as taking jabs and swings. Babe watched in amusement. He tried to swipe the big guy's legs from underneath him. Attempt failed. Babe let him dance around, throwing empty swings and jabs. Chop opened his fist, making contact with a slap across the face. Stung, but barely. The smaller man ran with all his might, wrapping his arms around Babe's torso to plow him down or twist him off balance. Nothing the man offered up did any good. Babe had not moved more than an inch. Chop came with a full roundhouse, hoping to make contact with Babe's jaw. The big man caught his wrist, stopping the blow.

"Chop, you done yet?" The helo man growled, pulled his arm away, ran full force into the stone wall of the massive body, and bounced off like a ball against the wall. "Give it up. I want to understand you because Collins' description while I served was considerably different. He said no one felt intimidated or uncomfortable around me. I was maybe quiet, but I got along well with the unit. I would have gladly taken a bullet for any one of them. For a while, the guilt ate me up, and I tried to eat my gun more than one time." He stood with his hands on his hips, head tilted like he was genuinely trying to understand. "You weren't in our unit, but we all held the highest regard for you and were grateful that you showed up in our time of need. We treated you like a brother."

Chop bent over, trying to catch his breath. The look of anguish on his face was foretelling. He had chosen option three to fight and made a fool

THE IMPOSTOR LIE

of himself. Now, he faced a torturous death. The big guy didn't have the slightest waver in his face. Chop pleaded his case. He whined that one of his sources for finding women called him and said he had a hot number that would fetch a high price. Chop reiterated that it would never have gone down if it had been prior knowledge of who the chick was. He asked what he should have said, like, 'Oh, my bad, I didn't know it was your girl. Never mind?' There was no way Babe would have let a comment such as that slide. He knew the Captain played by the rules, never doing drugs, getting drunk, or womanizing. Everything he did was as ordered and by the book. Failure was never an option. Babe shook his head, saying that could not have been farther from the truth. He lost Marines; he took bullets tearing through him. Babe emphasized that nobody knew the lives any of them had before the Corps. Maybe his had been shit, but enough of the talk.

"Ya know, it was common knowledge that I had a soft spot for your unit. I didn't have to do some of the things I did and, in fact, was written up once. You treated me like I was less than your unit and assumed I always had your back. You're welcome, by the way." Chop became red in the face, his eyes tearing up with heavy-duty emotions. He tried to run. Babe grabbed him, threw him to the ground, and torqued his neck. He gave him a much better death than he deserved. He left, closed the door behind him, and took off in the white truck.

Babe drove close to Claiborne, wiped the white truck down, and walked. With his glare and enormity, no one hassled him. He saw a vet with a sign that said, "Will work for food." Babe handed him fifty dollars and told him to get a meal and ride to the VA for help. He continued to walk and found himself at the job site on Conti. It was near completion and beautiful. Glenn was standing outside the trailer.

"How's it going, Babe? Whatcha think, beautiful?" Glenn seemed enthusiastic about having Babe stop by. "I've been keeping up to date through Bethany about Trinity's progress. She appears to be improving. What's your take?" He put his hand on Babe's shoulder. *Oh God, here goes the chummy BFF shit.*

Babe stepped toward the building. "Time. It will take time and hard work, but she'll get there. Show me around. When I think of the rubble disaster it was in the beginning, this is amazing. I bet Antoine is happy."

After a full narrated tour, Glenn invited him into the office. "So, what have you been up to? Want to return to work? We have another project that is getting ready to start. Look, I know Bethany interfered when she shouldn't have—"

Babe looked to the side, controlling his emotion, "No shit." He paused, "I get it, but that was one cluster fuck." *Change subject.* "How's the wedding coming? Y'all have been ready to go for months now."

Glenn took out two cups and poured bourbon into each. "We went to the justice of the peace, with her parents and mine witnessing the ceremony. When Trinity is back on her feet and able to dance, Antoinette has planned a storybook reception, complete with a Cinderella carriage. Hopefully, Bethany will be pregnant by that time." They both sat with their feet propped up, sipping the bourbon. Babe showed pictures of Chancée and expounded on fatherhood. Glenn ate it up. They touched on baptism, a thought the big guy never considered. And yet, another conversation with Trinity.

From the job site, Babe hailed a cab home, grabbed his truck, and headed to the hospital. Arriving at her room, he found she wasn't there. Confused, he asked the nurse. Thoughts binged in his mind like a pinball machine. Did her parents pull another underhanded maneuver? Much to his relief, she was in the gym on the first floor. The heat from his neck and the tightness of his muscles began to subside. Was this going to be the norm with them? Confusion shrouded his mind.

His phone lit up with a call from Javier. Reluctantly, he answered. "Marine, that pesky issue resolved?" Babe knew he was referring to Tim "Chop" Faraday.

"Yes, sir. I'm walking into P.T. to see Trinity. I'll have to call you back." Call ended. Trinity had the braces on but walked between the bars without holding on. Babe beamed, "Look at my girl. Your progress is amazing." The therapist said it was miraculous; he'd never seen anything like it. *Hmm. Antoinette and the Rosary.* "Do you mind if I work out while she exercises?"

"I'm supposed to say you can't, but looking at you, I think you know your way around physical training equipment, but if someone comes in, stop immediately." The therapist slowly walked behind Trinity. "This time, we are going past the end of the bars. I have your belt; you're safe." She felt unsure but took a few steps. "You'll have to tell Justine about our progress. She bragged about you squeezing her hand. This walking is way major. I'll be boasting about getting you out of the bars." He teased.

"Want to see something amazing? Watch my husband for a few seconds. Now, that's spectacular. See why I'm so horny? Who wouldn't want a piece of that?" She watched him and misstepped, but the therapist had the belt, and she was back into the rhythm of walking. "Did you ask the doctor?" She double-raised her eyebrows. "You know about the sex and positions?"

The therapist had a full-on blush and answered he had, and systems were a go, but carefully. Trinity teased back with a completely inappropriate response. He called Babe and said it was time to return to her room. Her mouth had made it impossible for him to do his job well. The therapist laughed but was obviously embarrassed. Babe rolled his eyes, asking what she had done or said. He nearly choked when Trinity chirped in with her comment. "Trinity, you and that mouth. You embarrassed that man and me. Girl, you slay me."

Once in the room, she asked question after question. How were the renovations to the gym coming along? How were the boys and Chancée?

What had he been doing? She said she could feel a difference in him and that it had filtered through the room. He seemed more at peace.

"I'm cracking the whip, and the workers are double-timin' it for your return home." While he never knew his grandfather did any physical labor, the space he had created for a workbench, tools, dolly, ladders, and the like made the perfect place for his exercise equipment and now for Trinity's therapy. In his mind's eye, he could visualize Jacob monkeying around with the chair lift and parallel bars. A warmth filled his heart. They had become a family.

Babe listened while Trinity regaled the gossip she heard from the nurse's station. The massive man was the highlight of many staff conversations, nurses and CNAs alike. He was the subject of most of the scuttlebutt. She commented that since the whole City Slasher mayhem and his picture on the television as the person who found him, the conversation had proportionately increased. She said she could hear them daring each other to approach her with questions of a more personal matter. Babe could feel the pink rolling up his neck to his ears and face. He chuffed, clearly embarrassed. Since the advent of life's feelings, Babe felt like a fish out of water. Hearing that they discussed his and Trinity's sex life brought a montage of visuals to the point where an adjustment was necessary.

"Vic, why don't you unzip your jeans and—"

"Girl, you must be crazy. Ain't no way, not here, not now." He shook his head as he spoke.

"But, look at you all ready for the taking." She giggled.

"Enough," he sternly commanded.

With an ear-to-ear smile, she saluted him, "Aye, aye, Captain Vicarelli."

Time flew when he was in the embrace of her eyes. She was witty, and her face full of expression. A quick call from Ruthie ended the chatter when she calmly asked him to please come home. "Gotta go, hot thing," he leaned over, kissed her, sliding his hand up her tee shirt to cop a quick feel. She squealed. "See you tomorrow. Behave."

THE IMPOSTOR LIE

The truck felt like it was on autopilot; he pulled into the driveway. Jacob came running out. "Quick, sir, please." In seconds, Babe was in the house.

Chris was laid out on the den sofa with garbage bags under him. Ruthie held a towel against him, and Reg had Chancée in the swing. A patch of blood grew from his abdomen. Chris tried to hold back tears, unsuccessfully. They trickled down his cheeks as he bit into his bottom lip, fighting the pain.

"What the fuck? Chris, what happened? Let me see." Babe pulled the boy's blood-drenched shirt away from his body and up. He had three puncture wounds that looked like they were from a knife. He hauled him up off the sofa, plastic bags and all, and drove like a bat out of hell to Touro. "When did this happen, Chris?" He could see the boy fading. "Stay with me, boy, do you hear me?" His voice sounded gruff. The ER didn't waste a minute to triage him; it was evident if they didn't get the blood flow under control, they were going to lose him. Stomach punctures could be extremely serious, especially with the propensity for them to turn septic, and then it was lights out. The staff rushed the boy onto a gurney and imaging and or surgery. The feeling was all too raw. As the doors closed behind them, blocking the view of Chris, bile gushed up his throat. He did not like being out of control.

Babe sat in the waiting room, flexing his fists open and closed. He hoped the son-of-a-bitch that hurt his boy was an adult, not a punk-ass kid, but whatever, he would settle the matter one way or another. A person from the hospital, probably registration, approached him. When their eyes met, there was familiarity. He remembered Babe. "I need you to come with me, please. I have to get the information on your son." Babe cleared his throat, thinking, *here we go again. How to explain the nature of their relationship. Was he the father? No. Was he the boy's dad? Resoundingly, yes. So, fuck anyone that didn't get it.*

The man asked for all the insurance information. Babe knew it was par for the course but wanted answers about Chris. The registration attendant, trying to ease the situation, commented. "I know I've seen you before, sir." He thought for a minute. "You are the guy who found the City Slasher, right?" Babe answered a quiet yes. "But, I think I've seen you before. I used to work at Universi—" he stopped talking. Babe's eyes seared through him. Yes, this had been the same man who had taken Trinity's information. The guy realized it. "Oh, God, I am so sorry," Babe answered, saying that she was recovering well and should be able to go home in a week or two. "Oh, thank God. I thought, well, never mind."

"Yes, I know, and yes, thank God." Once again, the God entity heard his prayers. "When will I know something about Chris?" The man held a finger up and pushed a few buttons on his phone. He asked about the boy and smiled, saying he would relay the message, but his dad would be waiting to speak to someone. The heavy weight on Babe's chest lessened, and he found his breathing stopped staggering. "And?" eyebrows lifted in question.

The gist and great news were the stab wounds had not damaged any vital organs beyond repair and that the GI system was intact. Babe thought, *one hurdle cleared*. Until he had the story from Chris, there wasn't much he could do but wait until the boy woke up from the surgery and was in his right mind. Babe called Ruthie with the good news. He heard her call out to the other two, and it was nothing short of jubilation. After hanging up, Babe sat in the waiting room with scattered thoughts bouncing in his head. He knew he'd had an abusive upbringing, and Babe knew some about two of the boys, but he was not privy to the boys' exact circumstances except maybe Jacob. Compared to them, Babe's was a walk in the park because of his grandfather. Fuck Gino; he'd gotten what he deserved, only twenty-five years too late.

A montage of pictures started in his head, beginning with Gino *when twelve-year-old Babe slammed him with the kitchen chair over and over. The scene changed in a blink: he was on the road with his unit. He'd been told it was safe and passed the search dog's detection. Trooper, a black lab, and his*

THE IMPOSTOR LIE

handler had missed one. With Mulaney only ten yards ahead, he was thrown but watched in utter disbelief as the explosion devastated Tiger Mulaney's right side. Even though he knew his Marine was probably dead, he crawled to him. Why hadn't he been in front of Mulaney? He should have been the one blown to pieces. God was not kind or loving. Why would He allow that? His other Marines held him back, but suddenly, the feeling of detainment became real, and four hospital attendants held him down.

Babe apologized, "I'm good. Let me go." They were not having any of it. The wreck he'd made of the waiting room was like a tornado had come through. It was a sheer blessing that no one else was in the waiting room.

A big black man close to Babe's size stated, "Not a chance in hell. I feel your pain, but have you gotten help? Or are you on any medications?" Babe's response was unimpressive; he wasn't on meds and had seen someone, but he was okay now. The stress of worry for Chris must have triggered his reaction. "What branch?" The man asked. Babe replied Marine. "I thought so. A devil dog can usually spot another." He tried to calm Babe down with soft, steady words. "Marine, we are going to hold you for observation." He tried to fight back, but they had him secured and were on the way to the psych ward. It was the best place for him; maybe he would get the help he needed. Babe tried to reason with them to no avail. Like it or not, he was there for at least twenty-four hours, if not forty-eight.

"I need to call my wife and the caretaker with my children. My wife is in a different hospital. Also, I need to be with my boy Chris when he wakes up from surgery." He didn't fight against anyone and showed respect and compliance. They brought him into a locked-down unit where they put not only the crazies but the criminally insane. *Fucking wonderful.*

The room they locked him in was maybe eight by twelve. He had handed over his watch, phone, belt, and laces from his boots. He kept a mental count of time. About an hour after the lock-up, the door opened. A slight man with wild grey hair and wireless glasses entered with the trusty clipboard and file held close to his chest. "Good evening, Mr. Vicarelli; I'm Dr. Burns." He wanted to correct him and say Captain, but those days had passed, and while he corrected other people, saying he was no longer a captain, he wanted to gain respect from the doctor. *Fair enough.*

Dr. Burns continued, "You were in the armed forces?" Babe answered yes, sir. The man was gentle and kind and looked Babe eye to eye. Babe saw the sincerity. "Do you struggle with memories of your time in combat?" The Marine responded that, at first, becoming a civilian had been difficult because of the lack of order, and the nightmares had been vivid, but once settled in, the nightmares drastically decreased, as did the hallucinations. He said the nightmares and such had quelled, and only when he was tired or stressed because of danger to a loved one did they appear and that it had been almost a year since his last episode.

The doctor jotted something in the file. "I see. Are you on medication or in therapy?" The response was a clear no, and he did just fine. At that point, he spoke about Ruthie and Trinity and said he needed to contact them immediately. He talked about Chris's surgery and said he wanted to be with him when he woke up. The little man nodded as though understanding. "Because of hospital protocol, I cannot let you wander the hospital on your own. I'm sure you understand. I would like to put you on a low dose of Ativan to see if it helps with your anxiety." He continued saying it would soothe the savage impulse in him, and perhaps he could check on his son with an escort at another time. He closed the file, smiled, and said it was nice to meet him. The doctor suggested that once stabilized, he should check in with the VA for counseling as they were the best equipped and knowledgeable about PTSD. The diagnosis made him cringe, but arguing would not serve any worthy purpose.

As the door closed, he heard the lock engage. He could have broken the little man in two, and it must have taken courage for him to enter the room with a reported insane grizzly who nearly destroyed the waiting room. If taking a small dose and they'd have to prove it to him would allow him to go escorted to see Chris, then so be it. Two hours went by. He started pacing, then calling out. "Hello? Anyone there? Stupid motherfuckers, I

THE IMPOSTOR LIE

know you're out there, now, get me the fuck outta here." With both fists, he pounded on the door.

Over an intercom, he heard someone say, "You are not helping your cause. Someone will be there soon."

"Soon, what the fuck is soon? My boy is in surgery; now get me the fuck outta here. Call the VA; they've given me clearance. Anything, but get me out."

The hospital had screwed down the few pieces of furniture in the room. There was no outlet to release his anger. He sat on the bed begrudgingly. He clasped his hands, bowed his head, and silently addressed Trinity's God. *Are you there, God? I need you to help me, please. Get me out of here. I don't want Chris to wake up and not have me there. Please, Lord God, Trinity tells me it is in your time; a quick response now would work. Merciful God, make something happen.*

Cal had been one of the foursome to bring him in. He spoke to the doctor. "I know this isn't my place, but you can't cage a Marine who has just had a breakdown. It'll drive him crazier, and he's likely to do more harm. Let me escort him to see his son; I promise I can take that Marine down if need be. He don't scare me none." The staff questioned the wisdom, but the doctor assented.

The military man who had been one of the four to put him on lockdown came in. He handed Babe his phone, returned his personal effects, and told him in precise terms that if he fucked up, he was more than capable of putting the Marine down, and there was no chance of him getting out, only jail time. The Ativan was a tiny pill, but they'd have to wait another twenty minutes in lockdown.

More questions. How did Chris end up with three stab wounds? What was he going to tell Trinity? He didn't want to upset her. Babe asked the attendant, "How long have you been out?"

"Ten plus years, but once a Marine," and Babe finished the line of always a Marine. "You?" The answer: two years and some. "Vicarelli, I didn't get counseling because I thought I could handle the beasts of memories like you at first. It was one helluva a mistake. The trouble was I couldn't. My girlfriend left me and took my child, saying I was a loser and fucking crazy. Civilian life is a non-stop circus of disorganization; that's why I had trouble. Yeah, I had hallucinations, but I also came back smokin' weed and trying anything to erase my memory. You're different." He stopped and stared at Babe. "You feel any calmer? I have to check your vitals before we can go down to recovery. Ya boy is out of surgery and in the recovery area. They will let you in, Doc Burns orders. Look, don't pull no shit with me; I'm as big and probably stronger with the same training as you, plus my job is on the line."

"I won't. Word."

Babe held out his arm. "Chief, you'll probably need the larger cuff. I usually run one-twenty over sixty, resting pulse around sixty." He passed the test. "I have to call my wife before I see Chris." The phone rang a few times. "Trinity, I'm at Touro with Chris." She responded in panic. "He's fine; I'll tell you everything as soon as possible." Silence. "I had an episode, and they put me in the lockdown unit—" Silence. "What do you mean good? Whatever, I'm not gonna argue with you. Yes, I'll see someone at the VA. Can you please call Ruthie and let her and the boys know Chris is out of surgery and okay? He will be in the hospital, I think, for a few days." She drilled him. "Pretty lady, I'm not getting into the details now. No. I love you and see you when I can. Keep working on it so you can come home."

With all the details taken care of, Cal escorted Babe to the recovery room. "Why's your woman in the hospital? She gonna be okay?"

Babe gave the gist of the story.

"Man, she's been in the hospital for a long time. She coulda died, ya know?"

Walking side by side with long strides, Babe replied, "Almost did several times."

THE IMPOSTOR LIE

The doors to recovery required a buzz-in. Evidently, the doctor had sent the word down because the doors magically opened. Chris was still asleep. Babe held his hand, leaning over, he said, "Chris, I got your back. I love you." The boy grunted, too.

HOME AT LAST

The hospital held Babe for seventy-two hours. The psych personnel determined Ativan was the charm. While unaware, the nurse or attendant had no clue that he hadn't swallowed it. A slight amount of the pill had melted under his tongue; in essence, he might have gotten a little of the effect, but more than ever, he needed to be at the height of his game. Chris' fight was still a mystery, and Babe had no idea how well Trinity was doing and when she'd be home. Dr. Burns discharged Babe with orders to seek counseling at the VA. The doctor had spoken to the shrink Babe had seen when he came home. The medical community planned to keep tabs on him. *Yeah, right.* He knew the VA was busting at the seams, and follow-up was a joke because the budget cuts from Congress took money away from the vets. *What a shitty thanks for your service.*

Within the same week, Babe, Trinity, and Chris were back home. Dinner became story-telling time. Ruthie sat with her mouth tightly pursed with the occasional thank you, Jesus. The first story told was about Trinity and the wild woman. It required a backstory, which Babe condensed into a few words but managed to convey the essence. He didn't get into his first encounter with Markey or that it was he that threw the rebar, but that the brother and sister were so distraught the sister attacked Trinity, nearly killing her. The pair disappeared forever. He didn't want the boys to be paranoid about the gruesome twosome.

The boys wanted to know what she remembered because she had been gone for such a long time, eight almost nine months. In typical unfiltered style, Jacob asked her if she'd ever be able to walk again without the braces. Babe cleared his throat and said she would, but it would take time. He nipped the conversation in the bud.

All eyes were on Chris as it was his turn to tell his story. He began, looking at his plate, almost disengaged. Was he ashamed, embarrassed, or hurt that a father could stab his own son? Babe watched each micro expression, and all he could read was confusion. The narrative didn't have inflection or emotion, more like the newscasters on television—the facts and nothing but the facts. The big difference between TV personalities and Chris was Chris' facts were true. "I was riding my bike toward Tchoupitoulas when a car pulled in front of me and stopped. A man got out and called me by name. It took a minute, but I realized it was my father. He looked homeless, not the buff guy I remembered. I told y'all that when he deployed, my mom hooked up with another man who didn't want me around, so I ended up on the street." Talking to Babe, he recounted, "Remember, I told the brat-pack you were a Marine, and I could tell cause of my dad?" Babe remembered the encounter and conversation.

"Anyways, he says, 'You look good, kid.' I said 'thanks' he says 'looks like you got some money' I said 'not much.' The bastard pulled a knife on me and tried to grab me off the bike. That's when he stabbed me. He lost balance, and the knife went in two more times. I don't think he meant to, but he did. Then he laid rubber and left. I made it a block from home when Reg saw me. He was on his bike and got me home. Ruthie saw me come through the gate, and I guess that's when she called you. Bastard! He was high, and I don't think he meant to hurt me. It was an accident."

Accident, my ass, Babe thought.

Trinity's mouth was open in shock. "Well, Chris, where does he live? Did y'all talk at all?"

Chris mumbled with a mouth full of pie, "Just what I said." Babe's mind started churning. If the man were indeed homeless, he would probably be under the Claiborne overpass, but he could be almost anywhere since he had a car. The big man tried putting pieces together; if Chris saw him near the river, he was probably somewhere along there.

Thinking to himself, Babe processed: Jacob's mom was a prostitute and died. The other working girls took care of him as best they could. He went on the street at about nine, so he hadn't been homeless much before the abduction. Chris's dad was in the military, and his mom picked up a new man. They put Chris on the street. Reg was still a mystery and he didn't want to discuss it, ever. He knew everybody's story but kept his hidden deep in his heart. *One day*, Babe thought.

Ruthie spoke up as the table quieted, "Sir, what's your story? Or is it too delicate to share?" She raised an eyebrow. *Doesn't she know by now I'm not like Javier?* He cleared his throat of the perpetual frog. It always happened when dealing with matters of the heart. He looked into the eyes of each person at the table.

"Y'all know I rushed Chris to the hospital, and they took him back to surgery. My e-emotions," he stuttered, "were all over the place. I started to think of y'all and the lives you'd lived, which made me think of my younger days and my abusive father. I snapped and had combat hallucinations. I caused such an uproar that they sent four attendants from the—" he looked away, then returned his focus to the table. "The people were from the psych unit. They told me I had PTSD. Do you know what that is?" They all said yes and that they'd known for a long time that he suffered from it. They had heard episodes in the middle of the night and were happy someone cared enough to get him help.

Trinity's eyes jetted to Babe, "What'd I tell you? Your boys love you and only want what's best. I told ya they knew." She batted her eyes at him sarcastically.

He pushed his arms down like he was trying to settle the sentiments from the air. "You were right." Ruthie let out a thank you, Gawd. She began clearing the dishes from the table. Reg got up to help. "No, sir. What is your story?"

"Not today, sir. Okay?" and he continued into the kitchen. Babe and Trinity exchanged glances. He'd let that one hold for a few days but was determined to find out. While Chris and Jacob's stories differed, they smacked of the same thing—they were on their own. Chris was sixteen, and Jacob was twelve when Babe took them in, but only they knew how old they were when the street became home. Two years had passed since they'd been with Babe, and Chris was on the brink of eighteen. The decision to go to L.S.U. had not changed. He'd become an avid watcher of college ball and would complain to the TV when he disagreed with a call or a play. They had become a family with love, fights, laughing, crying, whining, acceptance, and, most of all, loyalty.

The family sat around watching TV, incessantly chatting, and then the questions poured out about the attack Trinity sustained. The boys dug deeper into the woman who pretended to be her and why she would do that; it only messed with Babe's heart. Who was she? Babe was gentle in his explanation, trying hard not to disparage Trinity's family.

Babe leaned forward, resting his hands on his knees, trying for closeness. "Guys, Mama and Papa Noelle were so upset; remember, they lost Chance not long ago. Trinity was on the brink of death, and they thought they might lose her, too. The stress was massive and made their judgment different, making them think with their hearts and not their heads. Trinity has an almost identical cousin. At that time, the doctors had predicted that she was dying. They got Angelette to pretend to be Trinity to patch their hearts and mine. They thought I might not let them see the baby. When hard times come around, people do crazy things that make little sense. We have mended feelings, and life will continue as it always does with Sunday Mass and dinner."

Ruthie sipped her coffee and said serious talk was over for the night. Jacob asked if Babe and Trinity might have another baby. "Jacob, that is serious talk and none of anyone's business." Then he laughed and asked if

Gunner would ever have puppies. "Gunner is a boy dog, you know that, so no, he won't have puppies." Ruthie tsked in disapproval at his silliness.

Jacob tilted his head. "Are you sure he's a he?" The other boys broke into side-splitting laughter.

Babe got up for a nightcap and turned to Jacob, "I know why you're asking. He doesn't have balls, um, testicles because I got him chopped." The three boys grabbed their crotches and moaned, poor Gunn.

"On that note, everyone," Ruthie said, "I'm going to bed."

The five stayed awake talking for another thirty minutes, turned out the lights, and went upstairs. Trinity settled on her electric lift chair. "Thanks, Babe, for getting the house renovated for me." He walked close behind her and grinned, telling her it was until she no longer needed it, then the fucker was coming out. The night closed on a happy note for a nice change—no hospitals, serial killers, or uninvited guests. Babe had it all again: wife, baby girl, and loving boys—thank you, God.

Once in bed, the conversation returned to another baby, the kind of future Trinity wanted, including what sort of work Babe had in mind. They snuggled with the warmth they both needed. He sleepily went through a list of options: maybe going back to construction with Glenn; there was always Jarvis missions rescuing trafficked kids, perhaps applying for Corps Reserves unless she had anything she wanted him to do in particular. "Ideas, ma girl?" The soft purr of her sleep brought joy to his heart. Slumber was a multitude of thoughts away. Trucking through his mind was Chris' dad. What sort of man would demand money from his son at knifepoint? Maybe he had a bad case of PTSD and needed a hand-up. Since his plate was no longer filled with hospital visits, serial killer chasing, or house renovations, his time was his own for a change. His new mission was to find Chris' dad and get him into VA. Daniel might be a good source. He fell asleep with dreams of the Reserves. Somewhere between donning fatigues and the wails from a certain baby girl, he peacefully slept.

Trinity was still snuggled under the covers when he retrieved the world's most proficient screamer. The aroma of Ruthie's coffee was tantalizing. Once downstairs, Chris handed Babe a stack of papers. "This is all the sh-stuff about graduation and reminders about Project Graduation. Don't freak out; that was part of the papers I gave you earlier this year. It's all cool, bro." *Bro? What about sir?* Somebody had gotten a bit too big for his britches.

"Coming up soon, and are you still sure about L.S.U.?" Babe glanced over the papers.

"Uh, duh. Yeah," Chris copped an attitude.

Still looking at the papers, Babe responded, "Boy, I think someone forgot where they came from; you don't want to get on my bad side, now, do you?"

Chris shifted from one foot to the other, "Yes, sir, I mean, no, sir."

Ruthie brought a cup of coffee for Babe and a water bottle for Chris. "Make sure you drink this before school and put one in your backpack. The heat can knock you for a loop. Stay hydrated, especially since your ordeal." She hurried back into the kitchen for the princess' breakfast.

Babe turned in the chair and faced Chris. "Do you have any photos of your dad?"

"One, but he don't look like that anymore. He's living in his car and shaggy-looking. Hang on, it's upstairs." He bolted up the stairs with a grumble from Ruthie and was down in a flash. "This was him." Babe could see a strong resemblance between Chris and his dad. It was a shame that so many vets ended up on the street after serving their country.

Babe smiled at the boy, "You favor him." Suddenly, his heart dropped at the thought of Chris and his dad reconnecting; where would that put Babe? Would it split their family? Whatever the case, he needed to do the right thing. He returned the photo to Chris, who muttered in an ugliness regarding his father. "Chris, you don't know his story. Hold your final decision if he has the desire to get better. War was mere savagery; our enemy was beyond inhumane. I've gone to see the psychologist a couple of times and already feel the tension of my demons detracting." Much as it felt like slings and arrows into his heart, he told the boy to give his dad one more chance. "What kind of car did he drive, or what was the color? Let me take a picture of the photo." The boy said he thought the car was black or dark blue and looked like his paw-paw car, but it wasn't a Mercedes. School beckoned, and so did the street for Babe until he heard a slight sound.

While it was a barely audible sound, Babe heard it as Trinity rode the lift down. His instinct was to help her into the chair, but he needed to fuel her desire for independence, so he sat at the table listening for any unusual sound, ready to react at a moment's notice. She rolled into the room and delivered a sweet morning kiss. "Big man, can you spot me for my morning workout? I'll spot you." She laughed. Her sassiness was back in form. "What are your plans for the day?"

His eyes had a soft glow as he watched her. She was beautiful and his. "I thought I might look for Chris' dad. Want to take the ride after working out?" He tried to sound upbeat and return to normal as much as possible.

"Maybe. It all depends on how exhausted I am. You push me harder than the therapists, and that's saying something: those slave drivers; besides, I want to spend time with Chancée and Ruthie. You know, have a girl's day."

The exercise routine had progressed; Trinity could lift more than ever, and strength was returning, albeit slowly, to her legs. He wondered how she'd do without the braces but was going to wait for her to bring it up. They spent an hour in the exercise area, both drenched in shimmering sweat. "Shower time, girl. You some funk-nasty." She let out a roaring laugh.

"You ain't no delicate flower, Mister." Once inside, she asked him to carry her up the stairs and not make her use the old people's chair lift. He brought her up the stairs." Once upstairs, she whispered, "Help me get my clothes off." Was she exhausted, or was she sending an invitation? He peeled her clothes off piece by piece. Her legs appeared to have increased in size, and he bet she could walk without braces, but it was hers to suggest. "Now, please carry me to the shower." She double-lifted her brows. "I don't need the shower chair unless you'd rather me—" No coaxing was necessary; he held her under her thighs. She barely wrapped her legs around him, which he supported with his forearms. "C'mon Babe, no more delicate touch. You don't need to power drive, but let me know you mean business, you big stud-muffin. That's what I told the nurses at the hospital. I told them you were a stud-muffin and perfectly hung."

Babe held her against the tiles. It brought back so many blissful memories. He performed with purpose but held back the primal being that wanted to ravage her. He placed her in the shower chair. "Did you honestly say those things, or are you teasing me?" She had a devilish glimmer in her eyes. Her eyes said it all. Yes, she had said that and a helluva lot more. "As your mother says, 'Trinity Marie,' stop misbehaving. Is there anything that is strictly between us?"

She looked up as though she was thinking. "Not unless you asked me not to tell anyone. Your private moments and what you've done are your tales to tell, not mine." Her answer was satisfactory. She respected his personal experiences. "I gotta get put together, and it takes me lots longer than it used to, so get dressed and be on your way to find Chris' dad. Ruthie and I will have a fun time together."

Babe drove around the industrial area, thinking maybe he'd parked in some vacant parking lot, then headed toward the Claiborne Canal Street overpass. He showed the picture to a few people, but no one recognized him. There were several veterans to whom the big guy handed money, but none had seen the man in the photo. He continued down Claiborne; the panhandling was worse than he'd ever seen—*a sign of the times*, he thought. Traversing the streets, he started driving along Convention Center Boulevard. The city had boarded up a few buildings, but one caught his eye where the indigent had removed some of the boards from one window behind a once lush garden transformed into overgrowth. A dark-colored Mercury Marquis was parked outside. *Yeah, that would qualify as a paw-paw car.* He pulled behind it and entered the derelict building. The stench of piss and shit was vomit-worthy. He tied his outer shirt around his face as best he could, leaving him in a clean white wife beater.

The place was a haven for strung-out, homeless occupants. He illuminated his flashlight despite being cursed at by most of the habitants. There wasn't any sign of the man, so he left, checking the car as he walked by. In the reflection, he saw a person approaching from behind at a formidable pace. Babe yelled, "Don't pick a fight you can't win."

"Fuck you. Get away from my car, or you'll wish you had."

Babe turned around and challenged, "C'mon, sport." The man came at him with a blade pulled. He moved out of the way, but the man twisted and kicked him in the back, throwing him off balance. Babe dropped his overshirt, freeing up both arms. He was ready to grapple with the man. The bum stood still like an animal in spotlights.

"You a Marine? What the fuck are you doing by my car? I was a Marine until I wasn't. We can go at it, or you can be a man and tell me why you're by my car." The man was still in rigid alert mode, just like Babe.

Like a predator ready to attack, Babe was on high alert. "You Chris' father? What kind of parent stabs their kid three times? We almost lost him. On basic principle, I was gonna put you out of your misery, but out of respect for Chris and the Marine Corps, I thought I'd try to get you help." The man stuck his knife back in its sheath and dropped his hands by his side. "So, I have your attention? My name is Babe Vicarelli. Chris and two other street boys have lived with me for almost two years." Babe relaxed his shoulders and put his hands near his front pockets.

The man sat on the trunk of his car and tilted his head. "I think it's nice to meet you, but maybe not, Vicarelli? I'm CJ, Christopher James. I got fucked up over there in a bad way, all over the Middle East. I never knew when I would take my last breath and didn't give a hearty fuck. My ex sent the Dear John, and it was over. She married someone else and had a new life. I thought Chris was with her, and she'd poisoned the father-son thing. I've never been a good dad. I was a good Marine, but I gave in to drugs and let it dictate my life. I can't get a job, but I only tried at first. I quit trying and gave up. I didn't mean to stab the boy. My hands were sweaty, and I fumbled. Thanks for taking care of my kid. I can't believe she put him on the street. Poor little guy; man, that's harsh." The guy came across as humble and honest. Babe's bullshit-o-meter didn't go off. "CJ, let's grab an early lunch on me, from one jarhead to another. Get in my truck. I promise I will do you no harm."

The guy agreed and they took a long lunch talking about their lives. Babe talked more to him than he had most people in his entire life. *Maybe therapy is working, or is it Trinity or God?* He explained about his PTSD and how he lost it and was now going to the VA. He talked CJ into giving it a try. "Vicarelli, I don't do pity parties or begging. I pick up odd jobs here and there and get meals at shelters." Babe told him about Glenn and how he hired the military, but first, he'd have to clean up. It wasn't charity, and he expected him to pay it back or pay it forward to another veteran shunned by society. Babe dropped him off at his car, gave him fifty dollars, told him to get a haircut, pick up some decent clean clothes, and talk to Glenn. When he got paid, he could either give him the fifty back or give it to another vet willing to try and improve his life or squander the fifty; it was his choice.

"CJ, what do you want me to tell Chris? Here's my number. If you want to help yourself, I'll lend a hand; if not, oh well."

"Don't tell him anything. He's way better off with you than with me." He tapped the door of Babe's truck. "Good luck, Vicarelli. I hope you work the nightmares out." He turned and went back to his car. What happened from then was up to the man, but Babe felt good giving him a hand up.

Babe hadn't been gone from home for more than ten minutes when Trinity cornered Ruthie. "Can we talk?" Ruthie followed her into the den. "Tell me about Babe and how he has been since the beating." Trinity sat ready to listen with a Diet Coke in her hand and Miss Chancée in the baby swing. She advised Ruthie, "Get you some coffee; I got a feeling this is gonna be a story and a half."

"Girl, you don't know the half of it. I will get myself some coffee and toast bread. You want some?" Trinity told her to bring a plate of it and the melty things for the baby. "You know that's right. When she sees other people eating, she has to have something for herself, or she pitches an almighty stink."

Once settled, Ruthie began explaining the harrowing phone call from Babe and how he sounded out of his mind, not the cool, calculated Marine. Day and night, she said he'd stay at the hospital, only coming home to shower and take a few bites, then right back. She continued that something must have happened because he started working out like a fiend, still going to the hospital but letting off some steam. "Hon, one night, Babe came home and poured drink after drink. He didn't get drunk, but I could tell he was upset. He told me they were taking the baby the following day and asked me to pray for the baby and you. All went well, and the baby was fine as could be, but you were on death's doorstep again. Once he knew the baby was fine, he started going to see her." She sat quietly for a moment, sipping her coffee, but Trinity could see she was thinking.

"How were the boys? They must have missed him." She took a swallow of Diet Coke but maintained her eyes on Ruthie.

"The boys were confused; they didn't understand. He was more contemplative than usual. That's his word, not mine; I think he goes into the Devil's Workshop. After months, he comes home one day with a woman who could've been your sister, but she was pretending to be you. I knew it, the boys knew it, even the dog knew it wasn't you, but Babe wanted to believe you were back, so he accepted it. I'd catch him looking funny at her. Somewhere deep inside, he knew. I later found out she was your cousin. Not to be offensive, but that little trollop doesn't hold a candle next to you." She paused, searching the timeline. "Babe was all geared up in his tactical clothes, but maybe it only lasted a week. That's when he came home with a pretty, pretty man. You met him, Javier. Nice man and sure nice looking."

Trinity sheepishly asked, "Were they all lovey-dovey like he is with me?"

With an adamant tone to her voice, she said, "Absolutely not. The girl was coarse, common. I'm sorry I shouldn't say that about your family." She put her coffee cup on the saucer.

Trinity rolled into the kitchen and brought out another Diet Coke. "You can say all you want," she hollered from the kitchen, "because she's gonna face the music when I get my legs under me again. I'm gonna kick her ass. I'll put money in the jar later." She rolled next to Ruthie and patted the lady's hand. "Thank you for taking care of him. I know you did, and you took care of the boys; heck, they're just as much yours as Babe's. I know my sister put Angelette up to it, but damn, I wouldn't do that to an enemy, let alone a cousin, no matter what. She may even have a man. I don't care either way; she tried to take mine. To think my parents went along with it makes me ashamed of them. How could they do that to Babe?"

Ruthie and Trinity played with the baby while finishing the laundry. Ruthie stopped midfold and asked, "Don't you think it's odd how Reg doesn't want to talk? Maybe he's a runaway and is afraid Babe will turn him in. Your husband would have to, I guess. The boy is growing like the other two. Jacob is physically sprouting like a weed, but he's much to himself and not as mature as he should be. He's fourteen now, ya know. Jacob never talks about girls with the other two. I hear all their kibitzing. Chris looks almost like a man now, especially since he's using the weights. You asked me if Babe and your cousin were like lovebirds; the answer is no, not at all. He didn't like her, and I think it was breaking his heart because if it was you, then the brain trauma changed your personality. He didn't care for her one little bit. But, ya see, I knew the first time I laid eyes on the woman. I didn't talk much to her because I knew she was playing some game to get his money or get a baby from him. Women will do all sorts of things to trap a man. It's pitiful." Trinity started to think she shouldn't have opened that door. She was ready to stop talking about Angelette; it turned her stomach.

"I'm gonna rest awhile if you could look after the baby." She rolled over to the stairs and transferred to the lift chair while Ruthie followed closely. At the end of the ride, Trinity said she had it from there; in other words, give me some space. She managed to get into the bedroom and bed. The tears began to flow. Being at home all day was not the life for her, but until she could figure something out, there was nothing else she could do. *Okay, so I'm throwing a pity party, I fucking deserve a little pity.*

Babe bounded up the stairs when he came home. "Don't tell me you are sleeping again, my beauty." He opened the door to find her sobbing. "Talk to me, Trinity."

Her head dropped to her chest, "I wish I woulda died; what I got is no life, and I know what you're gonna say; give it time, Trinity." She said with a sing-song sarcastic inflection. "Everyone says that, fuck everyone."

Babe raised an eyebrow. "I'm not everyone, and I get it. Wanna hear about Chris' dad?" He tipped his head with a smirk.

She looked like a sad little girl, with tear-filled eyes and trembling bottom lip. "I should, but not right now; just hold me, Babe. Tell me it's gonna be alright." He lay beside her on the bed and pulled her close. She curled in a ball against his body. He kissed the top of her head. The room was still; the only sound was a slight whir from the ceiling fan.

The same thought echoed through his head, which inspired an internal debate. *I want to try to get her to walk. How can I put it?* Like the ding of an oven timer, the idea sprung to life. "Ma girl," he climbed out of bed and stood on her side. "You trust me?" She nodded with a look of indecision. "Do you?" Reluctantly, she nodded. "Stand in front of me. You know I won't let you get hurt." She sat perfectly still with a determined look not to stand. "C'mon, girl, if you trust me, stand in front of me." She swung her legs over the side of the mattress, closed her eyes, and let her body slide down the side with her feet touching the floor. She reached out for him. "You are fine, I'm here. Stand for a few seconds, then take a step." He stepped backward, ready to grab her, but he felt confident she'd be okay. She tightened her eyelids so tiny wrinkles were in the corners and took a step. She stood without moving for a few seconds, then took another step. Her eyes popped wide open as she stepped again. The big guy smiled ear to ear with tears trickling down his cheeks. "You are the most courageous person I know, Miss Trinity Marie. I'm so dang proud of you." He wrapped his arms around her and lifted her back onto the bed.

"No fuckin way, Babe. I can walk, dammit, so I'm going to walk. Just around the room with you in front of me and maybe down the hall." She walked around the room and then into the hall. Reg came out of his room and beamed when he saw her walking.

"Hey, y'all, can we talk? I told myself that once your fair damsel started to walk, I'd tell you my story. Are you ready to hear it?"

Things To Think About:

The adventure continues with Trinity, Babe, and their menagerie of kids and animals. They have the same stomping grounds, plus maybe one or two more. They've earned a break from the madness of their lives with one disaster after another. The questions to consider:

What about Reg?

Will CJ try to establish a bond with Chris?

Does anything happen with Trey and Max regarding their new captain, "Big Jim," and curiosities about Babe?

Does Trinity ever go back to work at Louie's Tap?

Is there someone in the background who penetrates Babe's secrets?

Discover answers to these questions in the sixth book in the **FIT THE CRIME** series, *The Impenetrable Lie.* *Visit my website:* corinnearrowood.com, for the latest scoop, my next thank-you party announcement, and freebie. I'd love to hear from you if you have questions.

As always, I wish you love, Corinne

Many Thanks

The more my writing progresses, the longer my list of acknowledgments becomes—so many wonderful people along the journey. I feel truly blessed.

I will always thank Doug, my handsome and loving husband of almost thirty-eight years. He is the love of my life, cream in my coffee, butter on my bread, as I am his. We're both like kids, just with many years of experience. Have I ever mentioned he is smashingly good-looking and ten years my junior? I was a Cougar before there were Cougars! *Thank you, God.* The bulls**t he puts up with me and my incessant questions is, I'm sure, taxing, but he never complains; he only says, "Wait, who did what?" Thank you for patiently waiting while I finish one more thought, which turns into a chapter hours later. Your support and encouragement give me the boost to continue my passion. There are two more books to finish the series, which is not a promise, just a maybe.

Thank you to our adult children and their husbands and wives for cheering me on, attending my release events, and inviting your friends. While I've known or met most of your friends throughout the years, having them as my readers brings us closer together, and I love it. The more, the merrier makes for a great party.

Thank you to our talented grandchildren, each making a mark on the world. Thank you for sharing that your Nana is an author. (I hope the three littles will follow in their older cousins' footsteps)

I don't think I've mentioned the Lunch Bunch. Bobbie, Kaki, Betsy, Susie, Kit, and the occasional surprise of Mary Catherine, y'all have been onboard with me since the first book. Great lunches, lots of laughs, and heartfelt conversation—Thank you, ladies, for your friendship and willingness to hear my constant chatter about new storylines. I love our Wednesday lunches, and one day, I will write *Tales of Time and Wisdom* delivered by the Lunch Bunch.

Thank you, Paige Brannon Gunter, for being the editor I need. Each time I finish a manuscript, I ask if you'll still take time for my book. It makes me nervous—what if she says she's too busy or its not her thing anymore? You've taught me more than you know. I can always count on your honest opinions and suggestions. You help me keep continuity in my books, catch the uh-ohs, and respond when I need a jump start. I love that you love the characters and appreciate their growth. Hopefully, you will be my forever editor. Have no fear; I will be your forever fan. Congrats on starting your own book. Woo Hoo!

Thank you, Kaye Chetta, for your rah-rah support and for being the second reader in the stable. Your support is invaluable. I look forward to more reading adventures together.

Thank you to Kristen Collura, who gathers friends from all over to my book signings and events.

Thanks to Karrie Mattia from the Book & The Bean for including me in many of her events and spreading the word about this local author. It was fun while it lasted—best of luck in your adventures returning to teaching.

Words cannot express my appreciation to Cyrus Wraith Walker. A fun fact—he's the one that found Captain Babe Vicarelli so that y'all can put a face (and body, yes, indeed!) to the name. He understands what I want as a cover design even when I can't describe it. You are absolutely amazing and bubbling over with talent. You are the real deal! Thank you for creating each book as a work of art. My study has all my cover designs you have done as artwork. Everyone loves my study!

I cannot express my appreciation enough to the readers who have followed my journey. I strive to quench your desire for adventure and relationships with my characters. I hope you enjoyed *The Impostor Lie* and look forward to Book Six, *The Impenetrable Lie*.

I offer my utmost gratitude to the men and women of the Armed Forces for their dedication, courage, and resolve to protect our country. It is with heartfelt thanks to the families and friends of our brave men and women of the Armed Forces, who sacrifice so much. Our prayers are with you and your loved ones. One of our grandsons, Brennon McWhorter, is in the Navy and currently deployed. Thank you, Bren, for your service and Godspeed. May He keep you safe in your journey.

The statistics of PTSD are staggering. Many of our Marines, soldiers, and sailors come home entrenched in the horrors they experienced and the nightmares they cannot escape. If you know one of our heroes who might be suffering from PTSD, contact the Wounded Warrior Project, National Center for PTSD, VA Caregiver Support Line at 888-823-7458.

Statistics show there are between 13 and 15 veteran suicides every day Pray for our men and women of the Armed Forces and support them as they return home. Get help from the Veterans Crisis Line. Call 988 (Press 1) or text 838255.

Other Books by the Author

Censored Time Trilogy
A Quarter Past Love (Book I)
Half Past Hate (Book II)
A Strike Past Time (Book III)

Friends Always
A Seat at the Table
PRICE TO PAY
The Presence Between

Fit the Crime Series
The Innocence Lie (Book I)
The Identity Lie (Book II)
The Impossible Lie (Book III)
The Inevitable Lie (Book IV)

Be On the Look Out for…
The Impenetrable Lie (Book VI of the Fit The Crime series)

Visit my website, corinnearrowood.com, and register to win freebies
Reviews are appreciated

About The Author

According to Me
Local girl to the core. There's nowhere on earth like New Orleans! I am still very much in love with my husband of over thirty-eight years, handsome hunk, Doug. I'm a Mom, Nana, and great-Nana. (four kids, thirteen grands, three great-grands) Favorite activities include hanging with the hubs, watching grandkids' games and activities, hiking, reading, and traveling. I am addicted to watching The Premier League, particularly Liverpool—The real football—married to a Brit; what can I say? I'm living my best life writing and playing with my characters and their stories. I'm a Girl Raised In The South (G.R.I.T.S.) Perhaps the most important thing about me is my faith in God. All of my characters, thus far, have opened a closed heart to an open one filled with Light. Some take longer than others.

According to the Editors
Born and raised in the enchanting city of New Orleans, the author lends a flavor of authenticity to her books and the characters that come to life in stories of love, lust, betrayal, and murder. Her vivid style of storytelling transports the reader to the very streets of New Orleans with its unique sights, smells, and intoxicating culture.